Death has a Cold Nose

When Linus Rintoul's current girlfriend ditches him very publicly indeed, he is grateful for the tactful intervention of Maud Egremont, an elderly, eccentric and very wealthy widow who is particularly pleased to make the acquaintance of a government vet because she breeds and exhibits Korean Palace Dogs.

Linus gradually realizes that Mrs Egremont makes great demands on her friends, but his efforts to distance himself are only partially successful due to the fact that so many of her fellow dog-fanciers meet untimely ends. Or is it just coincidence that they all sold Mrs Egremont a dog? His own position isn't much helped by the suspicions of George Upperby, Mrs Egremont's son-in-law, who tells the police that Linus is after both Mrs Egremont's money and her daughter, George's wife.

Again and again, Linus is drawn back into the net on one pretext or another until Mrs Egremont asks him to meet her at the neolithic flint mines known as Grimes Graves. He soon discovers that they are all too aptly named . . .

JANET EDMONDS

Death has a
Cold Nose

THE CRIME CLUB
An Imprint of HarperCollins *Publishers*

First published in Great Britain in 1993
by The Crime Club, an imprint of
HarperCollins Publishers, 77–85 Fulham Palace Road,
Hammersmith, London W6 8JB

9 8 7 6 5 4 3 2 1

Janet Edmonds asserts the moral right to be identified
as the author of this work.

A catalogue record for this book is
available from the British Library

ISBN 0 00 232451 2

Photoset in Linotron Baskerville by
Rowland Phototypesetting Ltd
Bury St Edmunds, Suffolk
Printed and bound in Great Britain by
HarperCollins Book Manufacturing, Glasgow

CHAPTER 1

'You're the most tedious man it has ever been my misfortune to get entangled with. All you do is go on and on about your bloody job and your bloody pictures, and what's your idea of a fun holiday?' The speaker's expansive gesture embraced the whole of the north Norfolk coast. 'To come to this—this *dreary* hole where there's nothing to do except listen to you and nothing to see except watch you opening and shutting your mouth like a dead goldfish.'

Her voice was not restrained, nor was she the least embarrassed by the surreptitiously interested audience who paused in their passing by, ostensibly to look at the North Sea.

Linus Rintoul was both stunned by the unexpectedness of her outburst and embarrassed by its public nature. Neither emotion was detectable in the self-control of his deliberately pedantic reply.

'Dead goldfish don't, by definition, open and close their mouths,' he said.

'Oh my God, don't you *ever* react?'

'I take it you'd like us to go home,' he went on, determinedly calm.

'Not us. Me. I'm going home. Now,' she fumed.

'You'll need me to drive you. We'll go back to the hotel and settle up,' Linus said.

'No, thank you very much. I'm going home on my own. If I have to, I'll take a taxi the whole way. You can finish the week off, for all I care. Who knows? You might find some benighted female who actually *enjoys* hearing about mastitis, foot-rot and Rembrandt.' She turned on her sandalled heel in a manner that Linus decided almost certainly constituted a flounce and strode off across the neatly clipped grass of the cliff-top.

The passers-by, satisfied that the North Sea hadn't changed much since the last time they saw it and that the deplorable scene was over, continued on their way, studiously not looking at Linus as they passed.

'Dear me, what an intemperate outburst,' commented a voice behind him. 'Not what one would call a lady. You're well shot of her, young man.'

Startled, because he had long ago given up even thinking of himself as a young man, much less hearing himself described as one, Linus turned. The speaker was an elderly woman who was sitting on one of the wooden seats provided at intervals along the cliff-top by the local municipality for the benefit of such as her. Elderly, yes, but not quite as old as she might have one believe, he thought. The high stiff-ened collar of her cream lace blouse must have been out of fashion before she was ten. The skirt of her well-fitting suit was almost certainly long and he wouldn't be a bit surprised to learn it was made of bombazine, whatever that might be. That said, there was no denying the overall effect was most becoming and he wondered if that was why she had adopted the fashion of her mother's day, if not even of her grandmother's. She smiled and patted the slatted seat beside her in unspoken invitation.

Linus accepted, if only because the longer he stayed here, the less likely he was to encounter any witnesses to Madeleine's little scene.

'Maud Egremont,' the woman said, extending her hand.

'Linus Rintoul,' he replied, taking it.

'Nice name. Unusual. Your wife?'

'No. Girlfriend. Ex-girlfriend,' he amended wryly.

'Were you very fond of her?'

Linus thought about it. 'I was beginning to convince myself I was,' he said. 'But I suppose I can't have been. If I had been, I'd be more upset.'

'You may find you are once it's sunk in,' Mrs Egremont commented shrewdly.

'Perhaps. Somehow I don't think so. To tell you the truth, I was more than a bit relieved.'

'You looked embarrassed to me.'

'Oh, I was embarrassed, all right, but at the manner of it, not the fact itself.'

'Ah. So you came here for what used to be called a naughty weekend—or week, in your case.'

Linus grinned in spite of himself. 'I suppose you could call it that,' he agreed.

'I thought one went to Brighton for that sort of thing,' she remarked. 'Or is Brighton *passé?*'

'I think the whole idea of naughty week-ends is a bit *passé*,' Linus said. 'People don't think of it like that these days.'

'You mean you didn't sign in as Mr and Mrs Smith?' She sounded disappointed.

'I'm afraid not. We didn't sign in as Mr and Mrs anything.'

'Another illusion shattered. But why pick Hunstanton? I mean, it's a pleasant enough place but it's not exactly dashing, is it? I don't think I'd even call it particularly romantic. Was it your choice or hers?'

'Mine—and I don't know why. Maybe it was a very Freudian choice. Maybe I subconsciously wanted to be shot of her and knew Hunstanton would do the trick.'

'Dear me, how very subtle! There's a nice little tea-room along here a bit further. Why don't I let you buy me afternoon tea?'

'I can't think of any good reason,' Linus said and stood up, offering his arm. He noticed as she rose that her skirt stopped just above her ankles, circa 1914. At least she didn't affect a bustle, he thought irreverently.

The tea-rooms to which she led him were entirely in character and very pleasant despite the unashamed fakery of the olde worlde interior. Lace tablecloths had been laid over longer, pale-blue ones (Linus wondered how great an effort had been needed to avoid pink) and a small pottery vase of sweet peas stood in the centre of each. The china was several steps up from that usual in such places, the genteelly triangular sandwiches contained smoked salmon-and-cucumber or egg-and-cheese fillings, the scones were unmistakably homemade—as was the strawberry jam and, while there was no attempt to serve clotted cream, at least its substitute was stiffly whipped double cream and not some spineless squirted swirl from a pressurized can. He was not at all surprised to have a choice of teas. It was the sort of place Linus probably wouldn't have come into on his own, and it was the sort that evoked the simple comment, 'Oh dear,' from Madeleine. Nevertheless he wasn't at all reluctant to be there and knew he would enjoy the food.

'Tell me,' Mrs Egremont began once the waitress had taken their order, 'would I be right in deducing from the remarks I overhead that you're a farmer?'

Linus smiled. 'No. You'd be wrong.' He had no objection to telling her how he earned a living but he sensed that she might prefer to make a small game out of it.

Mrs Egremont appeared to be considering. 'Well,' she went on, 'mastitis could equally well refer to people, which would make you either a gynæcologist or perhaps an obstetrician but I don't think people suffer from foot-rot.'

'I imagine it's not very often recorded in humans,' Linus agreed, 'and you're right—I'm neither of those things.'

'So you must be a vet,' she concluded with an air of triumph not entirely commensurate with the difficulty of the problem. 'I don't understand where Rembrandt comes into it.'

'I like paintings. Sometimes I buy. It wasn't an interest Madeleine shared.'

Mrs Egremont raised an eyebrow. 'I knew veterinary

practice was profitable,' she remarked. 'I had no idea it could be as profitable as all that. A West End practice, I imagine.'

Linus laughed. 'No practice at all, as it happens. I'm a government vet. I work for the Ministry of Agriculture.'

'So you're just a pen-pusher.' She sounded disappointed.

'Not at all. Well, there's quite a bit of that, of course, but there is in anything nowadays. No, I spend most of my time out of the office. We inspect stockyards and slaughter-houses, advise farmers—that sort of thing.'

'And you can think in terms of Rembrandt? My, the civil service has come a long way.'

'You may safely assume that Rembrandt was a figure of speech,' Linus assured her. 'He's probably the only artist whose name Madeleine could remember. Even a vet in a private West End practice wouldn't be able to think in those terms and I certainly can't.'

'But you can afford to buy.'

'Sometimes—on a relatively small scale and not in-frequently with the cooperation of my bank manager. I've no other major calls on my purse, you know. That's one of the great advantages of being on one's own.'

'Hm. So where did what's-her-name—Madeleine—fit in? I shouldn't have thought she was a necessary accessory for a man who saw advantages in being alone.'

Linus smiled wryly. 'I suppose one jumps at opportunities to test the theory,' he said.

'I see. In rather the same way that one goes on banging one's head against a brick wall because it's so much nicer when one stops.'

'Something like that,' Linus agreed.

'So you're not a great advocate of learning from experience?'

'I prefer to think of myself as a latter-day Robert the Bruce,' Linus told her. 'You know: try, try and try again.'

'A glutton for punishment.'

'Or a classic example of hope springing eternal.'

'You think so? I'd prefer to quote Shaw: a triumph of hope over experience.'

'Well, I'm certainly not a very good judge of character,' Linus said. 'When I saw a little old lady sitting demurely on a bench, I didn't realize she was such a cynic.'

'Realist,' Mrs Egremont corrected him. 'And thank God you don't go in for euphemisms.'

Linus frowned. 'Euphemisms? Sorry, you've lost me. What euphemisms?'

'That's my point—there weren't any. I am what you said: a little old lady. I am not middle-aged or mature or a senior citizen and for some reason "old age pensioner" —which I have been for years—is no longer an expression people like to use. I can't think why.'

'It's not politically correct,' Linus told her, grinning. 'You can't call people "black" any more. They have to be "people of colour"; the blind are "visually impaired"; people who don't grow to normal height for whatever reason are "vertically challenged", which makes it sound as if they could do something about it if only they set their minds to it, which they can't. Anything which the majority regards as undesirable is now wrapped up in euphemism so that those using the euphemism can disguise their dis-taste and appear "caring". That's a very politically correct word, too. I saw you as a little old lady—which is, if you think about it, an historic inevitability for fifty per cent of the population. The rest will be little old men.'

'Quite right—and when you reach that state you'll find there are all sorts of advantages. You can say and do more or less whatever you want and get away with it. You no longer care what anyone thinks, and if they think anything at all—which I sometimes doubt—they just assume you're a bit dotty. It's quite relaxing.'

'No disadvantages?'

'Oh, there are always those. They're just different at

different stages of life. One is prepared for one's teeth to fall out, one's sight to get a bit wonky and one's hearing to go—I must compliment you, by the way, on speaking very clearly. I don't always catch what people say. But I wasn't prepared for the diminution of physical strength.'

'You expected to be able to go on humping hundred-weight sacks of coal?'

'No, of course not. Don't be silly. I mean I didn't expect to have to change my cast-iron cooking pans for aluminium. I wasn't altogether prepared for the vultures, either.'

'Vultures?' Linus, still thinking of physical disabilities, had momentarily lost her train of thought.

'Human vultures. Taking a rapid inventory every time they visit in case you've sold a bit of silver or given away —been conned out of it, they call it—the Crown Derby. Being nicer than they really want to be in the hope that if they're not in your will, you may change it, and if they are, you won't decide to cut them out.'

Correctly assuming she was referring to her own family, Linus was shocked. 'I'm sure you're exaggerating. Your cynicism's making you paranoid.'

'Realism,' she corrected him again. 'And I'm not—exaggerating or paranoid, I mean. You'll find out for your-self one day. A vet, you say? Why aren't you in private practice?'

Linus was happy to have the subject changed. Mrs Egre-mont might be as unperturbed by thoughts of vulturine relatives as she appeared, but Linus found it an uncomfort-able field of contemplation.

Briefly and in a deliberately matter-of-fact manner, Linus explained that he had been, once, but that the unsocial hours hadn't fitted in with the social ambitions of his wife who discovered, after he made the move to the civil service, that her ambitions were then thwarted by the much lower salary. Experience had taught him that a prosaic, unemotional tone was essential if his audience was not to conclude he felt sorry for himself.

Mrs Egremont heard him out in silence and then nodded knowingly. 'Hence the bit on the side,' she said when he had finished. Coming from her, the expression had the added impact of incongruity.

'If there's no longer a marriage, I'm not sure there's a side to have a bit on. Is there?' he asked.

She considered the point. 'I suppose not. Except, of course, that you didn't actually explain that there was no longer a marriage. Death or divorce?'

'Divorce.'

'I thought that was it. I won't say I'm sorry because I can never see the point in apologizing for something over which one had no control and, in any case, since it doesn't seem to have been a particularly successful marriage, it's probably just as well it ended.'

Linus sighed. 'Thank God for someone with a refreshingly logical approach. Most people think they've put their foot in it by asking and then get all embarrassed at a reply which they must have known was on the cards.'

'That's because they ask the question to fill a silence rather than out of genuine interest and they haven't the brains to work out the likely answers before they open their silly mouths. Believe me, if they found you were a widower, they'd be even more embarrassed, though what alternative endings to a marriage there can possibly be, is beyond me. People just don't think.'

Linus raised his teacup towards her in a toast. 'At least you're not one of them,' he said.

She smiled. 'I try to make the most of what the good Lord gave me,' she replied and then returned to the subject of his work. 'I don't suppose a government vet has much to do with dogs?'

Linus, usually astutely aware when someone was leading

up to free veterinary advice, mistook the question for con-
versational currency.

'Not very much. We inspect quarantine kennels and
that's about it.'

'You must have had quite a lot to do with them before
you went into the public sector.'

'Of course. Even in rural areas these days, small animal
practice is increasingly important.'

'And lucrative. I imagine it must be a lot harder to con
large sums out of a farmer than out of a besotted pet owner.'

'Farmers certainly watch the pennies, that's for sure.'

'I have Korean Palace Dogs, you know.'

'I didn't,' Linus said, seeing the quicksand too late. 'I
didn't know you had any dogs at all.'

'Goodness me, yes. Can't imagine being without them.
Korean Palace Dogs are real charmers—very strong per-
sonalities.'

'Most of the oriental breeds have that reputation,' Linus
commented.

'I suppose they do.' Mrs Egremont sounded surprised,
as if she hadn't thought of it until now. 'But these are
particularly special. You really ought to come and see
them.'

Linus murmured something about time, and the need,
now that Madeleine had left, to return home.

'Nonsense,' Mrs Egremont said bracingly. 'Now you've
got the opportunity to enjoy yourself properly, why throw
it away by going home?'

Linus refrained—with some difficulty—from commenting that giving a free veterinary opinion on someone's
dogs was not quite his idea of enjoying himself properly.
'Perhaps I could have a few days in Cambridge,' he said
doubtfully. Cambridge had the merit of being some distance
from Hunstanton which, charming though it was and Mrs
Egremont's dogs notwithstanding, did not really have much
to offer a man on holiday on his own, even a middle-aged

man with relatively modest criteria as to what constituted enjoyment.

'Cambridge? What has Cambridge to offer?' Mrs Egremont said scornfully, dismissing several centuries of cultural excellence. 'No, I'll tell you what we'll do. I won't take up any more of your time today. I've done what I set out to do, so you can go back to your hotel and—'

'Hang on a minute,' Linus interrupted. 'What do you mean—you've done what you set out to do? Do I infer from that phrase that you had some ulterior motive in talking to me?'

'Well, of course I did.' Mrs Egremont's surprise was genuine. 'I overheard—not that anyone within half a mile could have avoided it—a man being ditched in an extremely public and embarrassing manner. I didn't know you from Adam. How was I to know you wouldn't immediately throw yourself off the cliff? I still don't know you well enough to be sure you won't but at least our little chat has lowered the temperature.'

Linus was unsure whether to be amused or annoyed. 'I think it was Madeleine who was suffering from the high temperature,' he pointed out. 'In any case, I'm not the suicidal type—and if I were, I'd at least have the sense to go to Beachy Head, where the cliffs are worth jumping off. If one's going to do something, one might at least do it properly. The most I could expect from jumping off these cliffs would be a broken ankle.'

'Very painful, broken ankles.'

'Undoubtedly, but rarely fatal.'

'Don't be difficult, young man.' She broke off and looked away from Linus, towards the window. 'Oh no, not George,' she said, to Linus's total bemusement.

'You've lost me,' he said but turned to follow her gaze just too late to see the object of it.

'My son-in-law. He's coming in.'

The man who approached their table was in his fifties,

greyhaired and with a vaguely military look that was probably due more to his neatly-clipped moustache than anything else. He paused beside them.

'No, I shan't join you,' he said, anticipating the courtesy
that hadn't been uttered.

'You haven't been asked to,' Mrs Egremont pointed out.

He ignored the inference that his premature refusal
placed him socially in the wrong. 'I was just passing and
happened to glance in. Who's your friend?'

' "Just passing"?' his mother-in-law echoed. 'Since when
have you "just passed" Hunstanton? And if you think
staring through the window and scrutinizing every table is
"happening to glance in", then all I can say is that your
understanding of the English language is very different from
mine.'

The man flushed. 'I wasn't too far away so I thought I'd
drop in and see you. You weren't at home and I guessed you
might have gone out for tea, so, since I was here anyway, I
decided to have a look in the most likely places.'

'I might have been visiting friends.'

'Yes, you might, but you're not, are you?'

'Well, now you've found me, what do you want?'

'Nothing in particular. I told you, I decided to pop in
on the off-chance. Just to make sure you're all right, you
know. Winifred worries.'

'Really? She hides it well. Much more likely you wanted
to check that I hadn't already kicked the bucket and you
might have missed out on something.'

Her son-in-law reddened, obviously needled as, Linus
thought, he had every right to be. His sympathy evaporated
with the man's next words. He glanced towards Linus.

'I certainly didn't expect to find that you'd taken up with
some sort of toy-boy. At your age it's ridiculous—and you
ought to have realized by now that you're a target for any
con-artist who happens to get a whiff of your money.'

'At my age,' Mrs Egremont retorted, 'I'm entitled to do

what I like and with whom and if I decide to give someone all my money because I like them, then that's exactly what I shall do.' She studied Linus dispassionately for a moment and then turned back. 'Besides, he's a bit old for a toy-boy, don't you think?'

'Not when one calculates that he must be a good thirty years your junior.'

'Just the right age,' she replied with deliberately irritating complacency.

'I shall tell Winifred about this,' he warned.

Mrs Egremont smiled blandly. 'I'm sure you will: she is your wife, after all. You did say you weren't staying? Don't let us keep you. I'm sure you'd rather be off.'

'You haven't heard the last of this,' her son-in-law said. 'We shall have to keep a closer eye on you.'

'You mean you'll actually encourage my daughter to visit me? Goodness me, however shall I recover from the shock?'

The man reddened further, turned on his heel and stomped angrily out of the tea-shop. Mrs Egremont, apparently unmoved, turned to Linus.

'You see what I mean about vultures?'

'You could have told him it was a casual acquaintance,' Linus pointed out.

'Yes, I could have done but why spoil his fun? He'd *much* rather think I was in the unscrupulous clutches of a con-man. Now where was I? Oh yes—why don't you go back to your hotel and have a nice, relaxing evening in the bar. I shall give you my address and I'll expect you for lunch tomorrow. As a vet you'll enjoy looking at my dogs and as a bit of a connoisseur you'll enjoy my pictures.'

Linus seriously doubted the first part of this prognosis but he pricked up his ears at the second part. 'I had no idea you were interested in art as well,' he said.

'Why should you? I didn't mention it. I don't run to Rembrandt, either. In fact, I have to admit, I'm not all that knowledgeable but I know what I like and I only buy originals—mostly of dogs.'

Linus wondered if she was being disingenuous. He was all too familiar with the fact that 'I don't know much about Art but I know what I like' usually meant Constable's haywain or white horses leaping out of waves. One of the girls at the MAFF office had bought a print of the latter and showed it proudly to Linus, commenting that it was very witty, didn't he think? He could see no wit in it and said so. 'Don't you see? It's a sort of play on words—white horses, the sea.' And since he still looked blank, she had elucidated further. 'Foam-capped waves are called white horses, Linus. The artist has put in *real* white horses and has them leaping ashore like waves. Can't you see that?' Linus had told her that he had seen that from the beginning but that he had considered it neither witty nor particularly original. He was, however, prepared to concede that both the horses and the sea were very life-like.

Still, he couldn't be that rude to Mrs Egremont whom he scarcely knew, and there was always the possibility that she had a very good eye indeed and her pictures might we well worth seeing. So he smiled.

'Thank you,' he said. 'I'd like that.'

The house blended in well with Mrs Egremont's wardrobe. A mile or two from the town, it was a large Edwardian residence, more than a villa yet not quite a mansion, built of mellow brick in a medley of styles put together with a flair that made them work despite the odds. It was the sort of house that middle-aged, middle-income passers-by wished they could afford to live in. The gardens, which extended to about half an acre and had once, Linus guessed, been much bigger, were mostly grass bordered with mature shrubs and trees, skilfully planted to disguise the regularity of the boundaries. The soaring grey-blue of a magnificent Atlantic cedar took his eye. It was a tree frequently planted in this area but Linus couldn't recall having seen a better specimen. There were no flowerbeds, the only dash of colour being in a raised border that divided a flagged terrace from the adjacent lawn. The overall picture was one of quiet affluence. Linus guessed that the original owner had been a successful local doctor or solicitor.

There was nothing inside to shake his initial impression. It was an interior both lived-in and cared-for. Most of the furniture was older than the house, of quietly understated elegance and indisputable quality, and there was rather too much of it, in the way that people can't bring themselves to get rid of favourite pieces. Only the carpets and sofas were modern. The former were unpatterned, dense and benefited from thick underlays; the latter were of simple traditional lines, upholstered in chintz and superbly comfortable.

The pictures were a disappointment. There were, for example, several Scottish landscapes in heavy gilt frames, all heather-covered hillsides and Highland cattle.

'My late husband inherited those,' Mrs Egremont said, catching his glance. 'I don't like them much, either. Come into my little hidey-hole and see some of *my* pictures.'

The hidey-hole proved to a sitting-room which was, by the scale of the house, quite small, but which Linus estimated to be at least as big as his own sitting-room and probably bigger. A small, hairy dog curled up in an armchair lifted its head as they came and muttered something suitably inscrutable under its breath. So far as Linus could form any sort of opinion about it at all, it was that it resembled a Pekinese gone wrong. Or, more probably, he thought suddenly, a Pekinese before the breed's characteristics became exaggerated.

'Take no notice of Frizzle,' Mrs Egremont commended. 'She's very old and all she ever does is grumble. Someone should have told her about growing old gracefully. I can't decide whether she's never heard of it or chooses to ignore the idea. Now that's one of my favourites,' and she directed his gaze to a small picture over the mantelpiece.

Kitsch was one word to describe it. Schmaltz was another. Linus wondered briefly why it should have been German—or perhaps the original source was Yiddish—that should have supplied two such apposite words.

'It's certainly very appealing,' he said with perfect truth.

It was, if you like that sort of thing. Linus didn't. It was the sort of subject Landseer might have tackled, only if he had, at least the technique would have been impeccable. It showed a bitch and her puppies, of vaguely spaniel type, gazing up longingly at a little girl who was eating from a bowl of something. Probably, Linus thought, bread-and-milk or curds-and-whey. The child had abnormally pink cheeks, golden ringlets and a blue frock. She was probably consumptive, Linus decided with savage satisfaction. The bitch appeared to have a most unusual shoulder construction and her puppies appeared to have no bones at all. Despite their prominence, Linus guessed that in the artist's eyes, they were there merely to draw attention to the little girl. The picture was an original oil, expensively framed. Linus thought it nauseous.

'Isn't it sweet?' Mrs Egremont asked and Linus couldn't deny that 'sweet' summed it up with some accuracy. 'I couldn't resist it and I know I paid too much for it, but I loved it so. Still, it's original and it's an oil painting. It won't depreciate.'

Linus refrained from asking what it had cost. This wasn't a matter of etiquette because he had a feeling she'd be only too happy to tell him. It was because, whatever it was, he was fairly sure his horror would be reflected in his face and might be all-too-accurately interpreted. Mrs Egremont might not have much artistic taste, but she wasn't a fool.

In terms of subject, it was without doubt the most nauseous of the pictures she had bought herself. The best was a painting of some kittens. The subject was still too twee for Linus's taste but both the composition and the execution were first-class. Of the half-dozen or so other pictures, most were the work of amateurs and their only possible value, in Linus's opinion, would be to people who happened to own the breed in question—most were of dogs —particularly where the subject was named, and, apparently, to Mrs Egremont.

Linus was surprised that someone whose surroundings implied a woman of some taste and discrimination should have a sentimental blind spot where pictures were concerned. It was a pity because she could obviously afford to buy much better ones than he.

'How long have you been buying pictures?' he asked.

She cupped her hand round her ear. 'I beg your pardon? I didn't quite catch that. "How long . . ." I heard but not the rest.'

Linus repeated his question.

'Not very long at all. About six years, I suppose. I didn't buy anything while my husband was alive. I quite often saw things I liked but we didn't share the same tastes. He always called them "chocolate-box pictures" or "furnishing tosh". Between you and me,' and here she leaned confidingly towards him, 'William was just a teensy bit mean.'

Linus nodded his comprehension. He rather thought that he and the late William Egremont might have more in common with each other than either of them had with Maud.

'Did your husband buy on his own account or was he content with what he inherited?' Linus asked.

'Oh, he had a small collection. I sold it when he died. Actually it proved to be not quite so small as I'd imagined —very little of it was on the walls. Not these walls, that is.'

'What walls? His office?'

Mrs Egremont roared with laughter. 'That *would* have caused a stir! No, they weren't the sort of picture anyone would put on their office wall. He had several of the bigger ones on the walls of his bedroom and some in his study—which was out of bounds to the rest of the household. Most were in portfolios—and quite a revelation they were, I can tell you.'

'The mind boggles,' Linus commented. 'Tell me more.'

'The auction house called them "erotic art". They were the sort of thing people of his generation thought of as "dirty", which they weren't. I suppose the modern phrase would be "soft porn". There was an Alma Tadema which was quite nice, and a Fortunino Mantania which was certainly a little risqué and some Russell Flints—originals, not prints—but they're almost respectable nowadays. I've even seen them on the walls of a restaurant. He had a couple of Beardsleys and several Japanese prints that the young man from the auctioneers called "pillow pictures".'

Linus smiled to himself. He wouldn't have bought such pictures himself even if he could have afforded them, but if he'd inherited them, he certainly wouldn't have sent them to the auction rooms—and neither would he have hidden them away. 'You'll have done quite well from their sale,' he commented.

'Staggeringly,' she agreed. 'I'd no idea people were prepared to pay so much for that sort of thing. That's the money I've been using to finance my own collection which, I promise you, is very different.'

That was not a statement with which Linus could argue. Poor William must be turning in his grave. The sale of his collection would probably not have upset him unduly, but the artistic use to which the money was being put was quite another matter.

'Now you must have a look at my dogs,' she went on. 'It's probably a very good thing you're *not* in private practice: at least you'll be able to give me an opinion untainted by thoughts of possible future gain. Come on. Most of them are out here.'

She led the way down the thickly carpeted passage to the them-and-us door—the heavy swing door that divided what would once have been referred to as the nether regions —in other words, the kitchen and utility area—from the rest of the house. The carpeting stopped at this door and the area beyond it was floored with the patterned ceramic tiles of a hundred years ago. Linus wondered whether the local history society knew of their existence.

They were, of course, an ideal floor surface for half a dozen dogs. Half a dozen variations on Frizzle tumbled themselves off the old armchairs on either side of the Aga and their over-long claws clattered across the tiles. The sound reminded Linus of a temp that MAFF had once employed at Marston Road. The girl had been inordinately proud of her long fingernails, fear of damaging which had seriously slowed down her typing, an activity characterized by precisely this clatter.

Linus did not lose his heart to Korean Palace Dogs. He found them eminently resistible. They had all the signs of infantilism that make old ladies in particular dote on certain kinds of dog. Linus did not see big, round, bulgingly prominent eyes as appealing; he saw them as predisposing their possessors to ophthalmic ulcers and entropion. The rounded skull might call to mind the human baby; Linus knew it predisposed the breed to open fontanelles. The drooping, feathered ears might add to the soulful expression; Linus saw them as harbingers of trouble, from ear-mites to grass-awns. Not, he felt bound to concede, that these particular dogs were likely to pick up the latter from the manicured lawns outside.

'Aren't they adorable?' Mrs Egremont said proudly and Linus was glad she had phrased it in a manner with which he could agree without perjuring himself: many people would have found them very adorable. His hostess might equally easily have said 'Don't you just adore them?' a phraseology to which it would have been harder to find a diplomatic reply.

The dogs were certainly pleased to see their owner though their interest in Linus was minimal: each one gave him a cursory sniff, decided he was of no account and transferred its attention to the person who really mattered. There seemed to be little wrong with them. In fact, given that their owner was a little old lady who clearly doted on them, they were surprisingly fit, being well-covered without being fat and having a musculature that suggested they had a great deal more in the way of exercise than pottering about in Mrs Egremont's garden.

'What seems to be wrong with them?' he asked.

'Nothing,' she answered. 'They pick up the odd flea, of course, but they're not ill or anything.'

'Then why did you want my opinion?'

'Do you think they're likely to be prone to any hereditary abnormalities?' she asked.

Linus was taken aback. 'I'm not the one to ask that,' he told her. 'Breeders will be able to tell you that. They're the ones who'll know what there is in their breed. I certainly can't tell by looking at them. Prominent eyes tend to predispose the dog to entropion—ingrowing eyelids—and that's hereditary, but apart from that I'm not in any position to comment.'

'It's no good asking a breeder,' Mrs Egremont told him scornfully. 'They'll tell you what's in the breed but always add that it hasn't cropped up in their dogs. Which is just what you'd expect them to say.'

'And what do they say crops up in the breed?' Linus asked, unable to dispute her last statement.

'Entropion—which you've already said—and luxating patellas mostly. That's slipping kneecaps,' she added, in case a government vet's education had skipped over that particular basic condition.

Linus nodded. 'That's quite common in small dogs,' he

agreed. 'Is that it? Entropion and luxating patellae?'

Mrs Egremont nodded.

'Then, if you want my opinion, the breed's in a remark-ably healthy situation if it's only got two hereditary abnor-malities to worry about. I can examine your dogs for both, if you like, but I have to say, watching them bounce like that, there's no hint of lameness at all.'

Mrs Egremont looked shocked. 'No, they've never been lame—and they'd go straight to the vet if they were. But he does think I'm a bit of a fuss-pot, though he's always very polite and no doubt the size of the bill eases his irri-tation,' she added shrewdly. 'I'd be grateful for your opinion.'

There was, Linus knew, a small problem of professional ethics here but since, as a government vet, he could hardly be accused of poaching clients and since there were also considerations of politeness to take into account, he had little hesitation in disregarding them. If he found anything wrong, he would tell her to take the dog concerned to her usual vet.

He found nothing. Even Frizzle, who growled continu-ously throughout an examination which she clearly regarded as an indignity, was as healthy as any twelve-year-old dog could be expected to be, even if her temperament could only be described as crotchety.

'They're fine,' he said when he'd finished. He allowed his glance to stray up to the shelf above the Aga. Several rosettes were pinned to a notice-board screwed into the wall behind it, a modern incongruity in a kitchen of William Morris tiles and scrubbed deal furniture.

'You show?' he asked.

'From time to time,' Mrs Egremont replied. 'When I get a new puppy, I show it for a year or two. Maybe, if it does well, even for four or five years. Then I don't bother until I've another new one. I don't want to be tied down to too many dogs, you see, and I don't want a houseful of pensioners so I tend to space them out so that there's a range of age here.'

'Very sensible,' Linus agreed. 'Do you ever breed yourself?'

She shook her head. 'I've thought about it but it would be silly. I'd never be able to bring myself to part with the puppies. William always said that would be a passport to disaster and although I hated him at the time for saying it, now that he's dead, I have to admit he was right.'

'It sounds to me as if your husband was a very wise man,' Linus commented.

'So I've been told,' she replaced and, although her tone was affable enough, Linus suspected that it wasn't an opinion she necessarily shared—or perhaps it was one of which she preferred not to be reminded.

'What I don't quite understand,' he went on, 'is why you're worried: if your own dogs are OK—and they are—and if you're not bothered about breeding, why should you be unduly worried about the general state of the breed?'

'I'm toying with the idea of getting another puppy,' she replied. 'I suppose I just wanted to satisfy myself that there've been no long-term bad results from the kennels I've been to previously.'

Her choice of words was such that Linus suspected she wanted him to demand clarification but he was disinclined to go on playing ball: he had repaid her hospitality with his free professional opinion, she would have to be content with that. So instead he got to his feet and made the goodness-me-is-that-the-time noises of someone who, while he may not have outstayed his welcome, wishes on his own account to be gone. Mrs Egremont's reaction succeeded immediately in making him feel guilty.

'How very selfish of me to keep you talking,' she said. 'Of course, you'll have things to be doing of far greater interest than listening to me moithering on.' As he opened his mouth to protest, sincerely, that that was not what he had meant, she raised her hand to stop his protestation. 'No need to be polite. You've been more than kind and, to tell the truth, I've enjoyed your company. You're a refreshing change, young man, though you may not realize it. I hope you enjoy the rest of your holiday. Or will you decide to call it a day and go home?'

Linus had been toying with the idea of doing precisely that. Now he prepared to change his mind. Norfolk had been less than fascinating largely because it had been quite the wrong place to which to bring Madeleine and because nowhere is so interesting when one is on one's own as it is in company. It occurred to him that Mrs Egremont was very good company. She was old without being remotely feeble; she was refreshingly forthright; and she managed to convey a shrewd common sense allied to a certain dottiness. He also suspected that despite her caustic remarks she was a very kind-hearted woman. He had to admit that he was quite glad not to live in the same county as she, but nevertheless he wouldn't be at all averse to spending a few more days in her company. Perhaps, he thought optimistically, he might be able to channel her artistic tastes into more worthwhile areas.

'No, I'll stay on a bit,' he said. 'I'll finish this week, if nothing else. Why don't I pick you up in the morning and drive you over to the Fitzwilliam? They're got a very famous painting of a dog that I think you'll like. We could have lunch in Cambridge and then home again.'

She looked puzzled. 'I didn't think the Fitzwilliam sold pictures,' she said.

Linus smiled. 'It doesn't, and even if it did, I think, with all due respect, that Gainsborough would be as much outside your reach as it is mine. But it's always worth going to look at the best. Gets the eye in,' he added.

'In the hope that eventually I'll stop buying sentimental rubbish. Is that what you mean?'

Linus was shocked that he had apparently been so transparent. 'Not quite,' he said, lying.

'Rubbish,' she said cheerfully. 'That's exactly what my son-in-law thinks only he expresses it far less diplomatically. He's very good at the pursed lips, the more-in-sorrow-than-in-anger shake of the head and the I-suppose-we'd-better-humour-the-old-biddy tone of voice. I'll probably enjoy a day out with you but wouldn't you rather be seen out with some dolly-bird on your arm?'

Linus grinned. 'Not in the Fitzwilliam,' he said. 'Besides, dolly-birds don't figure very prominently in my life. In fact,' he added, considering the matter, 'I don't think I've ever been out with one.'

'Obviously a deprived existence,' she remarked with a noticeable and, Linus suspected, deliberate, lack of sympathy.

'Quite. I shall have to start brooding about it. What about tomorrow? Is it on?'

'Oh, definitely. I've always fancied a toy-boy.'

'Always?'

'Well, ever since someone explained the expression to me. In my youth they were called gigolos. Not nearly such a nice word.'

'And I think with slightly different connotations,' Linus said, un-offended. 'I'll pick you up about nine. That'll enable us to get to Cambridge in time for coffee.'

The purpose-built, prefabricated garage was at some distance from the house. Linus had swung his car in front of it and parked in such a way that his back had been towards the garage when he got out of his car. Now that he was walking towards it he could see that the garage door wasn't entirely closed and that something inside gleamed.

'Do you have a car?' he asked Mrs Egremont who was escorting him back to his.

She looked surprised. 'Of course. It's essential these days, don't you think? Actually this one's really rather splendid. Move yours forward a few yards and I'll show you.'

Linus did as he was bid and when he got out of the driving-seat, found she had opened one of the garage doors.

'Don't you just love it?' Mrs Egremont asked.

Linus confessed that he did, indeed. The car was an old Armstrong-Siddeley Sapphire and it gleamed in midnight blue and black. 'Does it go?' he asked.

'Of course it goes,' she replied indignantly. 'It takes me shopping when it's raining.'

'And do you drive?' It seemed a silly question, but it occurred to Linus that he hadn't so far seen anyone—companion, housekeeper, or even a daily woman, who might also have acted as chauffeur.

'My dear boy, I've been driving cars since the 'thirties,' she replied, amused. 'William was the one who didn't drive. I had to be chauffeuse. I got hold of a chauffeur's cap once and put it on when we set out for somewhere or other. William was *not* amused. Mind you, I'm not so willing to drive very far these days. The roads are a lot more crowded than they used to be, you know.'

Linus agreed that they must be and took a loving, lingering look at the Sapphire before getting back into his mud-spattered bottom-of-the-range estate. He told himself as he drove away that the Sapphire was not environmentally friendly. It was a reflection that did nothing to diminish his covetousness.

CHAPTER 2

Cambridge was a success. Mrs Egremont clearly enjoyed it enormously and Linus enjoyed it so much more than he had expected to that when Mrs Egremont asked him to come to tea next day, he had no hesitation in accepting.

'I'm not inviting you to lunch,' she said bluntly, 'because although I've had a marvellous time today, I know perfectly well I shall be . . . what's the word for it these days? . . . knackered. Yes, knackered . . . tomorrow. So I shall spend all morning and half the afternoon in bed.'

'Then perhaps I'd better not make you get up at all,' Linus suggested.

'Nonsense. It'll do me good. Give a focal point to the day. Not before four o'clock, mind. But I'll be expecting you after that.'

There was a car in the drive when he arrived, and it wasn't the Armstrong-Siddeley. Mrs Egremont evidently had other visitors—or an other visitor—and Linus hesitated briefly in case he should be *de trop*. Then he reminded himself that he was expected and parked behind it. It was the sort of car that was bought as much to build an image as to get from A to B with the minimum of inconvenience and cost. It was unimaginative in design and far from cheap. It wasn't eye-catching enough to appeal to a yuppy and the sort of person who wanted such a car and could afford to buy one, probably made little use of the power under the bonnet. It wasn't a car Linus lusted after—unlike the Armstrong-Siddeley, and that was largely for nostalgic reasons—but he had to admit to a little smidgin of envy for the income that could afford it. It was a not inconsiderable comfort to remind himself that if he did not from time to time satisfy his lust for one picture or another, he too might be driving a car in a similar price bracket and not a very ordinary estate that looked older than it was because it was on the roads—more often than not, unmade roads—virtually every day of the week.

The front door was opened by a woman who, Linus judged, went with the car. In her mid-forties, she eschewed such vanities as tinting her pepper-and-salt hair and wore a short-sleeved shirt-waisted dress whose sole concession to femininity lay in its fabric: a floral Liberty print. With this she wore an unobtrusively good gold watch and a single strand of graduated pearls which both dated and aged her. Linus suspected the pearls were good, too. The picture was completed by sensible white sandals and Linus guessed there was a white handbag in the drawing-room.

He smiled. It wasn't easy and it wasn't returned. 'Linus Rintoul,' he introduced himself. 'Mrs Egremont is expecting me.'

'She mentioned it. You'd better come in.'

More gracious welcomes had been extended, Linus thought.

Mrs Egremont looked decidedly pleased to see him. 'Ah, Linus,' she said. 'You've met my daughter, Winifred. This is her husband, George Upperby. George, this is Linus Rintoul. You two have already met, of course.'

The man who had stormed out of the tea-rooms stood and extended his hand. His whole stance was wary and Linus guessed that the hand was proffered because it was expected and not through any innate good will.

George went with the car. Older than his wife, his grey hair was as well-tended as was his neat military moustache. He was dressed with studied casualness in a style that, had it been adopted by a con-man, Linus would unhesitatingly have diagnosed as phoney-Major. The shirt was cream, the cravat paisley silk, the cufflinks gold. The trousers were cavalry twill, the jacket a quiet houndstooth check and the shoes superbly polished brogues. Taken together with Winifred and the car, the image was complete. That wasn't to say it was necessarily false. George's military experience might, or might not, have been limited to his national service, but Linus had no doubt at all that the image the two Upperbys projected was the one they sincerely felt was theirs. In which case, he thought suddenly, can one really castigate it as an image, an expression which implies deceit? Well, there's always self-deception, he decided, though, to be fair, it sat more easily on Winifred's shoulders than on her husband's, perhaps because she had been brought up with money which Linus suspected George hadn't. He took the reluctantly offered hand.

'How d'you do?' he said.

'Come and sit here,' Mrs Egremont commanded, patting the sofa beside her. 'Linus is my toy-boy,' she explained to the others, with a malicious glance at her son-in-law.

Any embarrassment Linus might have felt was mitigated by the sudden realization that his hostess was enjoying the discomfiture of her other visitors.

'*Mother!*' Winifred protested. 'You'll embarrass Mr Rintoul.'

'Nonsense. He's unembarrassable. Aren't you?' Mrs Egremont added, turning to Linus.

'No, I'm not. And I don't think I'm a toy-boy either, but if it amuses you to call me one, I'm not about to get my knickers in a twist over it.' He turned to the other two. 'Do you live nearby?' he asked. 'I don't think Mrs Egremont has ever mentioned that.'

'Not as far away as some people might like,' George said severely, and Linus was unsure whether 'some people' was a reference to him, to their hostess, or both. 'We've a house on the outskirts of Thetford.'

'Ah, yes. Thetford,' Linus said. 'The refutation of Coward's epigram about Norfolk's being very flat.'

'You know it?'

'I've been through it. I intended to visit Grimes Graves but I haven't got around to it.'

'You haven't missed much: they're just holes in the ground. Well, not even that so far as the visitor's concerned: only one of them is open to the public and from what I've heard all the rest were filled in by the men who worked there, anyway.'

'Then I shan't bother. Thetford struck me as a nice little town, though. Is your business there?' It was a shot in the dark. Somehow Linus guessed that George's money came from business in the sense of trade rather than profession.

George Upperby allowed himself a satisfied, almost smug, smile. 'I'm a gentleman of leisure now,' he said. 'Sold out and decided to retire. Lets me concentrate on Council work.'

Linus correctly deduced that this meant George sat on, rather than worked for, his local Council. He didn't waste time asking which party he represented. 'Interesting,' he said and hoped his voice gave no indication that he found it the precise reverse.

'George was an ironmonger,' Mrs Egremont explained with a satisfaction that was clarified by her son-in-law's reaction.

'Hardly that, Mother.' He turned to Linus. 'I had a chain of hardware shops right across East Anglia.'

'Hardware!' his mother-in-law exclaimed disparagingly. 'Why use American euphemisms when there are perfectly good English words for it? They were ironmongers, and none the worse for being called that.'

'No one calls them that any more,' Winifred remarked mildly.

'*I* do,' her mother retorted with finality. 'Now Linus is a vet. A professional man,' she added to drive her point home.

'A successful practice?' George asked.

'No practice at all,' Linus said. 'I work for the government. I'm good at my job so I'd say I was successful, wouldn't you? I've never judged success by the mere accumulation of a bank balance.'

'No?' George was politely disbelieving—and the politeness was somewhat strained, Linus thought. 'You won't find many people of like mind these days,' George went on.

'Possibly not. It's not something I shall lose any sleep over. I've been ploughing my own furrow for a long time. I dare say I'll go on doing just that.'

'Linus has been looking after me very well these last few

days,' Mrs Egremont interjected. 'I've seen more of him in the last week than of either of you in the last year.'

'Don't be silly, Mummy,' Winifred said. 'You know we come over quite regularly—and if you weren't sometimes quite rude, we'd probably come over more often. You shouldn't give the impression we neglect you.'

'We like to keep a close eye on her,' George explained to Linus. 'As you must have noticed, she's not exactly a pauper and old people are so terribly persuadable. She's got some odd ideas, as it is.'

'My hearing may be dodgy,' his mother-in-law snapped, 'but it hasn't gone altogether, you know, and I'm not a half-wit. What's more, I'm still here—in this room as well as in the land of the living. Don't talk about me as if I were elsewhere.'

George was instantly contrite. Or rather, Linus amended, he slipped into the contrition mode. 'I'm sorry, Mother. Of course you're still here—and very *compos mentis*. It's just that we wouldn't want your friend to get the idea that your family neither knew nor cared what happened to you.' He turned back to Linus. 'And are you local?'

'Far from it,' Linus replied and thought his interlocutor relaxed. 'I work from Oxford. I'm just here on holiday.'

'So you'll soon be leaving us?'

'I think that's a reasonable assumption. Civil servants aren't like managing directors: they can't extend their holidays at will.'

'No, of course not. Not that a business can be left to run itself, you know. Those that are, soon run themselves into the ground,' and he chuckled at his little play on words. He was obviously not averse to having been described as a managing director as distinct, presumably, from an iron-monger. He was equally obviously very happy indeed to learn that Linus's stay was likely to be a brief one. His attention returned to Mrs Egremont and a change of sub-ject. Linus guessed that George Upperby was too shrewd to let his mistrust of Mrs Egremont's 'toy-boy'—who it now appeared was a temporary fitting—create a barrier between the old lady and her nearest relatives. 'And how are the dogs, Mother? We don't seem to have seen much of them today.' He turned back to Linus. 'Normally they're all over us, yapping like mad and snagging Winifred's tights.'

Since the dogs, with the exception of old Frizzle, had not been loose in the house during Linus's visit, he could only assume that they were one of Mrs Egremont's more effective weapons against her son-in-law, if not her daughter. He said nothing.

'They don't like you,' Mrs Egremont said. 'So when I saw you coming up the drive, I shut them up.'

'Hm,' Winifred snorted. 'Pity you've never shown quite so much consideration before.'

'I don't usually see you arriving,' her mother explained.

'No, but then we don't usually drop in unexpectedly, do we?' her daughter retorted. Match point to Winifred, Linus thought. In thirty years' time she would be a carbon-copy of her mother but at least she didn't seem to find it quite so necessary to placate the old woman as her husband did.

'Do you still have them all?' George persisted.

'I do. I'm afraid not one of them has dropped dead since your last visit, and Linus has had a look at them and says they're perfectly healthy.'

'That must have been a comfort to you.'

'I'd have been very surprised if they hadn't been,' his mother-in-law snapped. 'Still, it's just as well: one wouldn't want to bring a puppy to a house where things weren't hunky-dory.'

'A puppy? Another one? Mother, do you think that's wise? I mean, you've already got more dogs than anyone in their right mind needs.'

'Are you suggesting I'm *not* in my right mind?' Mrs Egremont demanded haughtily.

'No, of course not. It's just that most people . . . well, one or two dogs would be perfectly reasonable but five is really a bit much.'

'Six,' Mrs Egremont corrected him triumphantly.

'All the more reason for calling a halt.'

'What George means and is too sensitive to say,' Winifred interjected, 'is that you're an old woman now. There's quite a good chance you'll see your existing dogs out—most of them, anyway. If you buy another one, it's something else to be sorted out when you die. After all, the dog may reasonably live for fifteen years.'

'So may I.'

'The odds are against it,' Winifred said bluntly.

'In any case, there won't be any sorting out to do,' Mrs Egremont went on, choosing to ignore her daughter's unpalatable statement of fact. 'You know perfectly well I've taken care of them.'

'All we're suggesting is that you should let the ones you've got grow old gracefully with you and then, if you're left with none and you really think you can cope with a puppy, then by all means get another one. Why, Winifred and I would be happy to take it when you . . . when it becomes necessary, and look after it.'

'Poor little sod,' Mrs Egremont said, uncharacteristically explicit. 'No, thank you: I'll run my life—and my death— my way, and to the dogs' ultimate benefit. And now, if you don't mind my saying so, you and Winifred have outstayed your welcome. I wasn't expecting you and I don't like unexpected visitors. You may go now, and when you want to come again, please be kind enough to telephone beforehand.'

'So we're still welcome?' George seemed more anxious than his wife.

'I don't believe in overstatement,' Mrs Egremont replied, 'but I know my duty. In fact, I'll go further and if you promise faithfully not to mention dogs when you come, I'll promise to see they're shut up before you arrive.'

'Magnanimous,' Winifred commented.

'Not at all, because I don't think you—or rather, George —can stay off the topic for a whole visit. And if he doesn't, I shall let them all come bounding in at once. Goodbye. Linus will show you out.'

This instruction was such a blatant provocation that Linus felt embarrassed for the first time since his arrival. To their credit, both Upperbys chose to ignore it and said goodbye to him, if not with warmth, then at least with civility.

'Now that was naughty,' Linus said when he returned to the drawing-room.

'It was, wasn't it? What a pompous ass that man is! Winifred would be quite a nice woman if she wasn't married to him. She's the one who could use a toy-boy.'

'Why did she marry him?'

'To annoy us. No, that's unfair. We certainly objected to George but for quite different reasons from those that make me object to him now. William didn't think he had a future. He was a clerk in an ironmonger's—a real, old-fashioned ironmonger's—and he vowed to William that he'd see to it Winifred didn't suffer materially as a result of marrying him. It would take a few years, he said, but he'd do it, and do it without expecting William to put his hand in his pocket. And to give him his due, he kept his word. The archetypal self-made man, that's George Upperby. The Victorians would have loved him.'

'But Maud Egremont doesn't.'

'I used to be able to see what Winifred saw in him—he had fire in his belly in those days. Now there's just whisky. He'd done well for himself, but it's made him pompous and self-satisfied, which I suppose would be justified if he'd achieved it all on his own, but he hasn't.'

'You mean your husband did help him?'

'William? Goodness me, no. William wasn't a Mason, you see. Had no time for them. Said they were an evil lot. He was absolutely stunned when he discovered that our solicitor was one. Very nearly took all our legal business elsewhere but, Mason or not, he's a rattling good solicitor, so William overlooked it.'

'What did he think about George becoming one?'

'He never knew. Winifred and I agreed it was better to keep it quiet. He'd have banned him from the house and that would hardly have been fair on poor Winifred. Mind you, there's no denying they look after their own. George got a disproportionate number of contracts to supply this and that organization with all sorts of things. I call it iron-mongery, just to annoy him, and he calls it hardware, but the truth is, the shops are the tip of the iceberg. He also went into the whole business of supplying the building trade. His major business was as a builders' merchant. And it was freemasonry that enabled him to be as successful as he was.' She chuckled. 'He didn't go much on you, did he?'

'Do you blame him? Describing me as your toy-boy?'

'He thinks you're after my money.'

'Are you surprised after that introduction? Besides, what makes you think I'm not?'

'I have an instinct for these things and I'm not often wrong.'

'That sounds to me dangerously like famous last words.'

'I don't think I'd be quite so sanguine about it if you'd been the one to strike up the acquaintance but it was I who spoke first. I don't think you were even aware I was there.'

'That's true enough. Just remember for future reference that con-artists are by definition not easily detectable. If they were, they wouldn't be very successful. And now, if it's all the same to you, I'm going to take my leave of you, too.'

'Oh dear. So soon? I thought you were going to stay a few more days?'

'Just back to my hotel. With all due respect to your relatives, I could do with some fresh air and a total absence of caustic comments and veiled innuendoes.'

'I don't suppose you fancy coming round tomorrow?'

Linus, who was beginning to think rather wistfully of the pleasures of a day spent entirely in his own company, said, 'Why? What had you in mind?'

'You know how it is when women get depressed: some of them go on shopping sprees, others gorge themselves on chocolate? Well, I buy dogs.'

'Isn't that rather drastic? Dogs have to be fed, watered, cleaned up after and taken to the vet for the next twelve years or so?'

'Oh, I don't usually do it unless I was thinking about it anyway. Which is probably just as well since visits from George always leave me depressed to a greater or lesser degree.'

'So what has all this to do with me?'

'I'd be grateful if you'd come with me. To give me your professional opinion, and all that.'

'You seem to have bought dogs without it before and done quite well.'

'Not really. I've never bought a puppy that didn't turn out to have *something* wrong with it, even if it was something easily put right.'

'For instance?'

'Worms, or an upset tummy—that sort of thing. And although I always buy a show quality puppy—or at least, that's what I say I want and what I pay for—they never do turn out quite as well as I expect.'

'My opinion isn't going to be of the slightest use in determining a puppy's show potential,' Linus pointed out. 'I don't know the first thing about it. As for worms and upset tummies, the first is easily treated and the second isn't unusual when a puppy changes home—and it's hardly the breeder's fault.'

'Yes, but I'm going to somebody new this time. She hasn't been breeding very long and I'm not sure she knows what she's doing. I'd value your opinion.'

'Wouldn't it be wiser to go to someone you've bought from before? There's not much wrong with the dogs you've got.'

She shook her head. 'No, I'd like to give this Sharon Dedham a try. You don't have to take me. I can always drive myself if you'd rather have a day to yourself.'

If it had been her intention to make Linus feel guilty for raising so many objections, she succeeded and he protested that he was perfectly willing to take her and to give the puppies the once-over.

On the way back to his hotel, he cursed himself for giving in to what was, after all, little short of emotional blackmail. He had no curiosity and little interest in a litter of Korean Palace Dogs and the truth was, he was beginning to feel more than a little suffocated by Maud Egremont. She was good company and in many ways very refreshing company because old age had released her from the inhibitions of not saying just what she thought whenever it suited her so to do. He couldn't deny that the acquaintance they'd struck up had annihilated at a stroke any depression or loss of self-esteem he might have felt as a result of Madeleine's very public walk-out, and Linus was grateful for that.

Nevertheless, Mrs Egremont was a very demanding old lady. She liked having someone dance attendance on her and it was possibly her wealth that led her to expect them to do so. Linus wondered why she didn't employ a companion and then wondered whether at some time she had done so but had been unable to keep one. After all, the days of near-destitute relatives of the maiden-lady sort must be long past and even the most tedious nine-to-five job would be preferable in most women's minds these days to being at the beck and call of a capricious old lady.

Linus had little doubt that Mrs Egremont could be very capricious indeed if it suited her.

No, he would take her tomorrow to look at these blasted puppies and then he would bring his holiday to a premature end. Or rather, that's what he would tell her. He still had several days—the better part of a week, in fact—due to him, so maybe he'd motor up to somewhere else, well away from East Anglia, for a few days. Northumbria was said to be rather beautiful and he'd never been there.

To think of Sharon Dedham's breeding activities as a kennels would have been to have quite the wrong idea. It would have been hard to find a less suitable environment for breeding dogs, even small dogs.

The Dedhams lived in a terraced house—Linus guessed an estate agent would have called it a town house—in a new town. The properties in the little close almost certainly belonged, not to the residents, but to a Development Corporation, if not to the local council. The front gardens were minimal and open-plan, which meant that any attempts to turn them into a pleasant feature were frustrated by the activities of the local children who were turned out into the street to play so that they could annoy the neighbours rather than their parents. The back gardens were pocket handkerchiefs. Modest pocket handkerchiefs. Linus was only surprised that anyone was allowed to keep more than one dog at all.

Sharon Dedham was a pleasant enough young woman who tried hard despite the odds. She was in her mid-twenties and Linus, who was no admirer of skinny women, though she could usefully lose a few pounds and get her hair professionally cut. Bedroom hair needed to be thick and lustrous as well as long. Sharon's was neither. However, both she and the house were clean and Linus could find no fault at all with the condition of the puppies.

Their whelping box had been placed under what was

meant to be the breakfast bar and now that they were well out of the nest, it still served as an indoor kennel. Mesh panels confined them to a run when Sharon didn't want them all over the kitchen but, since the kitchen floor was covered with old newspapers, he guessed they spent more time out than in. The appliances here and the furniture in the sitting-room had the indefinable look of having been bought second-hand but the bedding in the kennel was the imitation sheepskin used by most breeders these days; there was plenty of it and it looked as if it was washed every day. The kitchen smelled of disinfectant rather than dog.

'This is Linus Rintoul,' Mrs Egremont said. 'I hope you didn't mind my bringing him. He's a vet, you see.'

'No, not at all,' Mrs Dedham replied, though it seemed to Linus she was a little taken aback.

'Have you been breeding long?' he asked, as much to set her at ease as out of interest.

'No. This is our second litter. The first litter has done quite well in the show-ring.'

Linus nodded. 'Do you show very much?'

'Not as much as I'd like. There's the cost, for one thing: it's becoming very expensive. And then, you see, I don't drive so I'm dependent on Kevin being able to take me. He's not all that interested and of course if he's on duty or called out, then I can't go unless someone can give me a lift. Still, I manage.'

'Called out?' Linus echoed. The phrase suggested a doctor or vet—quite at variance with the surroundings.

'Kevin's a motor mechanic. He works for a firm that does a lot of motorway recovery work. The money's good but he earns every penny. We're saving hard to be able to move out to the country somewhere where I can keep dogs without having to worry about neighbours.'

Mrs Egremont's attention had been given entirely to the

puppies but now she glanced up at Linus. 'Well?' she demanded. 'What do you think?'

'There's nothing wrong with the puppies, so far as I can see,' he replied. 'In fact, I'd go further and say that so far as their health goes, they're a credit to their breeder. I'm not prepared to comment on their show potential because I just wouldn't know, but I've already warned you about that.'

'How many of these are already spoken for?' Mrs Egremont asked.

'None. I've got several people wanting one but I promised you first refusal, so you take your pick and they choose from the rest.'

Mrs Egremont nodded and Linus guessed not only that this was what she had expected but what she had become accustomed to. It was one of the privileges of wealth.

She had narrowed the choice down to two and was carefully weighing up the pros and cons of each of them, while Mrs Dedham added her own opinion without, Linus noted, trying to influence the older woman one way or the other, when they heard the front door slam.

'That'll be Kevin,' Mrs Dedham said.

Linus did not warm to Kevin Dedham. If the man spent the better part of a day underneath a car, no one would expect him to be clean, but Kevin Dedham was also surly to a point just short of outright rudeness—and probably restrained himself from that only through fear of losing a sale.

'I did tell you Mrs Egremont was coming to choose her puppy, today,' his wife said by way of introduction.

'Thought she'd have made her mind up by now,' he commented ungraciously.

'All the more credit to your wife's puppy-rearing that I haven't,' Mrs Egremont told him sharply.

He chose to ignore the comment and turned to Linus. 'Your car or hers?' he asked.

'Mine. Why?'

'Just wondered. Won't be long before it comes my way.'

Linus refused to be wound up. 'More likely to break down in Oxfordshire,' he said cheerfully. 'That's where I live.'

Kevin grinned humourlessly. 'Pity. I was just thinking I could offer you a special rate.'

'If I break down in your area, I'll remind you of the offer.' Linus turned to Mrs Egremont. 'Have you decided yet?'

'I do rather like the little bitch but dogs are showable for longer and this little brindle dog is really very nice. How much did you say?'

'Three hundred and fifty for your pick of the litter,' Kevin said quickly before his wife had had time to do more than open her mouth.

Mrs Egremont pursed her lips. 'That's high, and you know it,' she said.

'Why not? You know the breeding's good or you wouldn't be here and you can see she's done them well.'

'I take it if something goes wrong—if I can no longer keep it, for instance—you'll automatically take it back?'

Kevin Dedham wiped an oily hand down the leg of his oily overalls. 'You have to be joking,' he said bluntly. 'Once it's bought, it stays bought. Once it leaves these premises, it's your responsibility.'

'We're talking livestock here,' Linus butted in. 'Not second-hand cars.'

'Business is business, no matter what,' Kevin replied. 'If she gets it home and then finds something wrong with it, I bet she'll be on to the Trading Standards people fast enough.'

'What I had in mind,' Mrs Egremont said, ignoring this exchange, 'is that in the sort of situation I was thinking of, the dog—which might be quite old by that time—would come with an income to cover his board and lodging until he died—always provided he were still living with your wife, of course.'

The prospect of having the dog back suddenly seemed considerably more attractive and Linus guessed the young man was probably rapidly evaluating various schemes by which the putative income could be turned to advantage without the drain of actually housing and feeding the dog concerned.

'Well, I dare say . . . in those circumstances . . . What d'you think, Sharon?'

'I'd want it back, anyway,' his wife said. 'I like to know where my puppies are.'

'Yes, but we've got to be realistic about it. We can't go giving blanket guarantees,' her husband warned her.

'I know we can't really afford it but on the other hand, they're only small. They don't cost much to feed.'

He snorted. 'It isn't the cost of food that's the problem. I didn't realize when I let you go in for this how much the vet's bills would set us back, not to mention entry fees and petrol.'

'Can't we talk about this later?' Sharon pleaded. 'As far as this puppy's concerned, Mrs Egremont's already said she'll see to it all that's taken care of. The thing is, she'll also show him, and I do need to get more of my puppies into the ring. That's the way to be sure of sales in the future.'

He shook his head. 'All right, so there's no problem over this one, but you've got to get one thing straight, Sharon: this is business and there's no room for sentiment in business.'

He brightened up perceptibly when Mrs Egremont paid cash, even though she very pointedly handed it over to Sharon and not to the husband who held his hand out for it. Business or not, Linus thought, that was three hundred and fifty pounds which was unlikely to find its way on to any books.

'Not a nice young man,' he remarked as they drew away from the curb.

'A thoroughly nasty piece of work, if you ask me,' Mrs Egremont replied. 'Sharon's all right. Her heart's in the right place. Goodness only knows why she chose to lumber herself with a character like that.'

'I couldn't quite make up my mind whether she's frightened of him,' Linus went on.

'He certainly browbeats her. I wouldn't be a bit surprised to learn he takes it a lot further than that. The story is that he's been to jail.'

'What for?'

'I don't know for sure. GBH has been mentioned but I wouldn't rule out that being pure speculation rather than hard fact. He's not popular among dog people.'

'That raises dog people one notch in my estimation,' Linus said drily.

'And you call me a cynic,' his companion remarked affably. 'Mind you, in a way you can't blame him for his attitude. They're very obviously hard up.'

'Then they shouldn't be breeding livestock,' Linus said severely. 'It's always a gamble at best. Breeding pedigree anything is a rich man's sport—or it ought to be because it's only the rich who can afford to tie a big enough knot before going on when something goes wrong. If you haven't got the financial resources, you tend to turn a blind eye to where you're going wrong.'

'You're being too severe,' Mrs Egremont told him and chuckled. 'Jolly good job I didn't tell him about my will,' she said.

'Your will?' Linus was startled. 'D'you mean Will with a capital letter, or without?'

'With, I suppose. From what we've seen today, coupled with his reputation, he's about the last person I'd give the details to.'

'I'm curious,' Linus said. 'I don't suppose you'd believe

me if I said I wasn't. What's in your will is none of my business but I can't deny you've whetted my curiosity.'

'Oh, it's no secret,' Mrs Egremont told him airily. 'There must be any number of people—mainly in dogs—who know all about it.'

Linus refrained from mentioning that in that case, if Kevin Dedham hadn't already heard, it wouldn't be long before he did. Instead he asked, 'Am I allowed to know, too?'

'Why not? It's perfectly simple. My first concern is for my dogs. They've given me a lot of pleasure over the years and I'm too sentimental to insist that they're all put down when I go. On the other hand, I couldn't bear the thought of them being passed from home to home and some of them will be pensioners by then and it's virtually impossible to re-home old dogs—people are magnanimous enough to give a home to a young dog if it comes free, but their magnanimity doesn't stretch to an oldie. So it seemed to me the sensible thing to do would be to leave them to whoever bred them, together with enough money to ensure they're kept till they die. So everything I've got will be divided equally between the people who bred the dogs I leave behind me, provided they take the dogs back and look after them till they die. If they can't or won't have them, then I'm afraid the dog is put down and the money goes to a hospice.'

Linus did some quick mental arithmetic. He hadn't always listened as carefully as he ought to what Mrs Egremont had told him about her dogs but he thought there couldn't be more than three or four breeders involved at most, and the most mean-spirited assessment of Mrs Egremont's assets added up to a very tidy sum indeed, even when divided by four. He didn't think the likelihood of the bequest's being turned down was very high. It was unlikely that Mrs Egremont hadn't come to the same conclusion. He was less sure that she had spotted some loopholes which had struck him. It was quite possible that what she had outlined to him was just that—an outline. Nevertheless, he felt something should be said.

'What check have you instituted to make sure the dogs *are* kept and aren't put down or given away as soon as the breeder has the money?'

She shook her head. 'They're not that sort of people.'

'Not even Kevin Dedham?'

'Ah.' There was a long pause. 'The money would actually go to his wife, of course, but even so . . . I take your point. I wonder . . . this is a great liberty but I wonder whether you'd take on the job of checking the dogs out at sporadic intervals?'

'I'd rather not. Quite apart from anything else, you hardly know me. You certainly can't be sure I wouldn't abuse your trust. In any case, to be absolutely frank, I wouldn't know one individual dog from another—and certainly not if I only saw it at yearly or even quarterly, intervals.'

'That's easy enough: I'll get all my dogs tattooed and you'd only have to look at the tattoo.'

While that would undoubtedly solve the problem of identification, it did nothing to resolve the underlying problem which was that Linus simply didn't want the job.

'I know what I'll do,' Mrs Egremont went on. 'I'll add a codicil giving you full veterinary responsibility for them and, since the breeders are fairly well scattered, I'll provide an annuity as well, so that you're not out of pocket. How does that strike you?'

'Very generous but quite unnecessary,' Linus said firmly. 'Your own vet is more than capable of carrying out your wishes. Better, in fact, because he knows the dogs and may even know which is which.'

'I doubt it,' she said. 'Besides, I like you. I'd rather have you do it, but if you don't like that idea, I've got a better one.'

She paused expectantly and Linus hoped his groan wasn't audible. 'Go on,' he said.

'I won't leave you an annuity. Instead I'll make the breeders responsible for paying your expenses and fee and arrange that they only get the income until and unless you agree that the dog should be put down. Then they'll get the capital. If they don't cooperate, you have the power to stop the money. That ought to keep them in line, don't you think? Especially if they know that the capital they've forfeited is going to be divided between the others.'

Linus agreed she had a point, though he forbore pointing out that it all hinged entirely on his integrity and while *he* knew he was honest, in all fairness Mrs Egremont had only a gut feeling that he could be trusted, and a gut feeling wasn't enough when the money involved was so well worth setting up a swindle. He suspected that there were other, less easily spotted, loopholes but contented himself with the thought that by the time anyone had the opportunity to slip through them, Mrs Egremont would be dead and therefore unaware of them. He still didn't want the job.

'What about your daughter and son-in-law?' he asked. 'Where do they come in all this?'

'They don't. Well, Winifred gets an ornament she's always liked because my solicitor said it was very unwise to leave her out of it altogether. William settled quite a sizable sum on her when he died and George has got plenty so they really don't need any more.'

'My acquaintance with the very well-off is somewhat limited,' Linus said, 'but I've noticed they're not usually averse to augmenting their little pile.'

'People very quickly become acquisitive,' Mrs Egremont said disapprovingly. 'Just because they *want* it doesn't mean they *need* it. Winifred and George will just have to put up with it.'

'Have they been told?'

'Oh yes. Years ago. They weren't very happy about it.

Mind you, I've a hunch they don't really believe it. I think George thinks I only said it to annoy him.' She chuckled. 'So I shall be proved to have done something that will give him pleasure for years,' she concluded.

'You've lost me,' Linus said, mystified.

'There's nothing George Upperby enjoys so much as good moan,' his companion told him. 'My will will have given him something really substantial to moan about for the rest of his life—and all his friends will commiserate with him. He'll be the happiest man alive.'

Linus doubted it. He also doubted whether George Upperby's understanding of his mother-in-law was quite as ill-judged as she chose to think. If George Upperby was as successful a self-made man as it appeared, then, help from the Masons notwithstanding, he was almost certainly a pretty shrewd judge of character. No wonder the Upperbys hadn't been overjoyed to see a male companion on the scene. Toy-boy or con artist, it must have made the likelihood of Mrs Egremont's changing her will in their favour even less likely. Linus had liked Winifred marginally more than her husband but he hadn't warmed to either of them. Nevertheless, he couldn't blame them for regarding him with some suspicion. In their shoes he'd have felt the same.

When they got back to Mrs Egremont's house, Linus was adamant. He was not going to inoculate the new puppy.

'You have a perfectly good vet of your own,' he said. 'I don't carry vaccine, anyway.'

'But you could get it.' She sounded almost petulant.

'Of course I could get it but I'm not going to. That really would be stretching professional ethics too far. Besides, you don't want to do it until the puppy's settled in and had time to get over the trauma of the move. If you're wise, you'll give it a week or two before you add another shock to its system.'

'You could if you wanted to.'

'Yes, I could. Only I don't want to, and for all the reasons I've given you before. In any case, I'm off home tomorrow and, with all due respect, I'm not traipsing all the way back here to inoculate a puppy, even if it wasn't unethical.'

'You're a very obstinate young man.' Her displeasure was evident in her voice and Linus wondered whether she was accustomed to getting her own way in everything.

'So my wife was always telling me,' he said, unmoved.

'I don't think I like you quite as much as I did.' It was like listening to a spoilt but highly articulate child.

'I'm sorry for that, but it doesn't alter my position. This is just something on which we'll have to agree to differ. It's probably just as well I'm off home tomorrow.'

'It probably is.'

Linus drove north to Northumbria with a sense of relief tempered with more than a little guilt. From now on there would be nobody to suggest, even in the nicest possible way, how he should dispose of his precious free time. He would stay wherever it took his fancy to stay; he would visit whatever sights he felt inclined to see; why, he might even walk along Hadrian's Wall. That had a nicely romantic, open-air, back-to-the-roots feel about it—walking Hadrian's Wall. He smiled to himself in the warm cocoon of the car. Hadrian's Wall would be windy, cold and the views would almost certainly be obscured by sheets of rain, if not enshrouded in mist. And he wasn't the open-air type any more than he was the walking type. The towpath of the Oxford Canal was one thing—and not only because it was liberally festooned with pleasant little country pubs. In any case, there was little point in walking if you didn't have a dog to walk with. He missed having a dog. Perhaps it was something he ought to think about remedying. Not that Hadrian's Wall was likely to be a very good place for walking a dog, anyway. Linus had never been there, but he had a very strong suspicion the surrounding moors would be full of semi-wild sheep—and sheep and dogs didn't mix. It was something to do with the nervous manner in which sheep moved. Even trained sheepdogs weren't always to be trusted when they weren't actually on the job. No. Maybe he'd drive out and look at Hadrian's Wall, but that was about as far as he'd get. It didn't matter. The point was he could do—or not do—exactly what he liked. There was no Madeleine with wishes to be taken into account and there was no Maud Egremont to take him over and make use of him.

He had no doubt that that was what she had done, though he doubted whether she herself would have thought of it in quite those terms and maybe he was even being a bit unfair to think of her like that. He certainly felt a twinge of guilt. In a way he had made use of her; her company and her caustic tongue had eased him through the hole in his self-esteem created by Madeleine's public rejection of him, and then repaired the damage to such an extent that he hadn't even thought of Madeleine for two days and did so now with neither anguish nor regret.

Maud Egremont was probably a very lonely old lady and that went a long way to explaining the almost claustrophobic effect she had on him. He was sorry to have parted from her in a somewhat strained atmosphere but, upon reflection, even that had its compensation: it made it extremely unlikely she would carry out her threat to include him in her will, even if she remembered having expressed the intention. Old ladies weren't noted for their elephantine memories but they were notorious for capricious changes of mind.

Back in Oxford, Linus's guilt won a partial victory and he dropped her a note thanking her for her kindness and hospitality and expressing the hope that she would continue in good health. He deliberately made no mention of dogs.

Several weeks later he had a chatty letter from her, the main purpose of which seemed to be to appease the curiosity Mrs Egremont was sure he felt about the puppy he had helped her to choose. He would be pleased to know it was doing very well indeed, she had called it Tigger, on account of the brindle stripes, and was looking forward to bringing it out, a phrase which Linus correctly interpreted as meaning in the show-ring. She hoped he would keep in touch.

Linus read the letter through and then re-read it very carefully. He had no wish to get entangled in a correspondence with Mrs Egremont, and not only because he didn't much enjoy writing letters. He didn't think this letter called for a reply and when he re-read it again the following day, he saw no reason to change that opinion. So far as keeping in touch from time to time was concerned, that was something which could be perfectly well catered for by a Christmas card and the occasional holiday postcard. He didn't often take a proper holiday, so those would be few and far between.

CHAPTER 3

Linus got his green wellies out of the car and put them on. The sun was shining now and the forecast was good but it had rained solidly the day before and although the mud of the car park was drying out fast in the sunshine and the brisk Fen wind, it still bore the marks of yesterday's softness and signs of the difficulties some drivers had had in getting their cars out.

He liked agricultural shows and the East of England Show was one of the best even if it was out of his professional catchment area. Linus had had a day owing to him and could think of no better way to spend it.

Held on a permanent show site, laid out for the most part as a grid of asphalt paths, each numbered for identification and with the stands located on the grass squares between, regular visitors no doubt found their bearings quickly. Linus found it confusing even with a map and ended up using the grandstand as his lodestar. Life was simpler that way.

Purists might object to the fact that a show with an exhibition of paintings, pottery and photographs as well as displays of farm machinery, each piece costlier than a Rolls-Royce and specifically designed for the open acres of Fenland farms, with stalls selling Mexican jewellery and African carvings as well as others selling cattle-crushes and hen-houses, was too eclectic to be rated as a true agricultural show. Maybe they were right, but the variety brought in the townies and that, in Linus's opinion was no bad thing. If they went home with some inkling of the fact that the countryside was a place of work, not just a source of chocolate-box tops, that animals were not necessarily things to go 'ooh' and 'aah' over, maybe the show would have done some good. Nature was, on the whole, pretty beastly and if you sanitized it too much, it would disappear. What, he wondered, pausing to let a string of tiny, gleaming Dexter cattle cross the path towards the collecting ring, did vegetarian conservationists think was going to happen to all the meat breeds if everyone took up their gospel? Vegetarians, he had observed, were usually middle-class townies who'd as often as not been brought up on stories in which hedgehogs wore little dresses and thieving rabbits little jackets and ties. Country children saw life as it was and quickly learned the art of ferreting.

He paused to enjoy the heavy horse parade that preceded the rare breeds and then on an impulse made his way to the separate section that was the dog show. He hadn't quite abandoned the idea of getting himself another dog and maybe he'd see a breed to take his fancy. In any case, he knew one or two people in dogs and who knew who he might not bump into?

A glance at the catalogue told him that none of today's breeds was likely to appeal to him. Linus had nothing against small breeds. They just weren't quite his cup of tea, and he seemed to have picked a day when small breeds predominated. Never mind. You never could tell. He had once known some people—keen German Shepherd owners in the days when they'd been called Alsatians—who in some moment of aberration had bought a Pekinese. It had lived with the Shepherds, walked with them and was treated by its owners as if it had been one, with the result that it was a fit, feisty bundle of muscle, a very far cry from the popular image of the breed.

It was a small step from thoughts of Pekinese to Korean Palace Dogs and the catalogue showed that quite a few were entered. He turned to the relevant page and saw Mrs Egremont's name. Judging by the age of her exhibit, she had entered Tigger. He hesitated. Did he really want to renew the acquaintance? But then, why not? He was only here for the day and he wasn't averse to finding out how the little tyke had turned out.

He made his way to the benching tent labelled B. It wasn't always easy to work out the order of one breed in relation to another but within a breed it was easy since dogs were benched in alphabetical order of their owners.

No one listening to the cries of delight with which Mrs Egremont greeted him would have guessed that they had parted on less than amicable terms.

'*Such* a long time since I've seen you.' She almost gushed. She turned to the woman benched next to her. 'Janine, you must meet Linus Rintoul. He's the vet I told you about. The one who came with me to choose Tigger.'

Janine Flatford was a pleasant-looking woman in her early forties. She dressed unobtrusively but well, with that degree of English understatement that suggests the effect is achieved by instinct rather than thought. She wore no make-up and as a consequence was rather colourless. Linus thought that some lipstick, at least, would have 'lifted' her general appearance. He wouldn't have been at all surprised to be told she was a teacher. 'You chose well,' she remarked.

'I didn't choose at all,' Linus said. 'I'm a vet, not a dog-judge. All I did was assure Mrs Egremont the puppies were perfectly healthy. She's the one who did the choosing.' He turned to the lady in question. 'Are Tigger's breeders here? What was their name? Something to do with painting.'

Mrs Egremont looked puzzled, Janine Flatford bemused. 'Dedham,' Mrs Egremont told him. 'Sharon Dedham.'

'I knew there was some sort of connection. Is she still showing?'

'Occasionally. Not as often as she'd like. The entry fees here are rather high and that awful husband of hers is out of work now, I believe.'

'I got the impression they were finding it difficult enough when he was in work,' Linus commented.

'Do you remember old Frizzle?' Mrs Egremont asked and when Linus nodded, she went on, 'I lost her a couple of months ago. Janine here bred her as well as one of my others.'

'You've been in the breed some time, then,' Linus said, glad that a superficial familiarity with the dog show fraternity over the last few years had taught him the right social chit-chat.

'About fifteen years,' she said, 'but I'm still learning.'

'Aren't we all?' he replied automatically.

He didn't care much for the couple benched on the other side of Mrs Egremont and a glance in the catalogue did nothing to alter his initial opinion. Mr and Mrs Chilton-Foliat. Linus had an ingrained working-class distaste for double-barrelled names which was probably unmerited and almost certainly due to such names inducing a sense of inferiority in others. Also in their forties, both were dressed in the uniform of the image they wanted to project, in well-laundered and rather-tighter-than-necessary jeans, topped in his case with a check shirt, the sleeves of which were turned back a studied half way up his forearm, while she wore a politically-correct Greenpeace sweat-shirt with the collar of a white cotton blouse to lessen the severity of the neck. They had identified their image with pin-point precision, with no hint of gold chains or sovereign-rings, but there was something about their whole appearance that told Linus it quite lacked the instinctive taste of Janine Flatford. He would be prepared to stake a month's salary —well, a week's—that their car was a Volvo estate, and probably a maroon one.

'Let me introduce you to Charles and Meriel,' Mrs Egremont was saying and Linus realized these were the first-names that went with Chilton-Foliat—and went very well: Piers and Annabel would have been just that bit over the top.

'How do you do?' he said. 'Does Mrs Egremont have some of your stock, too?'

'Just one. Maud bought one from our first-ever litter and did quite well with it a few years ago,' Meriel told him. 'We owe her quite a debt of gratitude, actually, because it was seeing that one in the ring winning that brought a number of prospective buyers to us.'

'I hope you give her a commission,' Linus said lightly.

Meriel looked shocked. 'We don't do that in this breed,' she said.

'It was meant to be a joke,' Linus said. 'As a matter of fact, I didn't know it went on in any breed, but I don't think anyone would suspect Mrs Egremont needed to collect commission.'

Mrs Egremont laughed, but mirthlessly. 'I don't, but I'll tell you this, young man: the ones who do expect a commission are precisely the ones who don't need it.'

'That's human nature,' Charles Chilton-Foliat said and no one felt inclined to quarrel with this platitude.

'Now there's two more people I want you to meet,' Mrs Egremont said, taking him by the arm and steering him further down the line of benches.

'Why?' Linus asked.

'Because they're friends of mine and I like my friends to know each other,' she replied in a tone of innocent surprise that told Linus as clearly as words that she had an ulterior motive. 'They're a very nice couple indeed,' she went on, 'and you mustn't hold it against them that they're gay.'

'If you think I might, why tell me they are?' he asked, annoyed. There were plenty of gay men in the dog game and, while homosexuality was not a condition Linus could either explain or understand, neither was it one whose existence in others bothered him one iota.

'You'd have to be singularly naïve not to spot it for yourself,' she said tartly. 'I just don't want them upset by snide comments.'

'I don't think I'm given to snide comments,' Linus said.

'No, you're not. That was unfair. I'm sorry.'

Julian Treorchy and Ted Blandford were a couple entirely conventional in every way except one. Linus wasn't surprised to learn that Mrs Egremont had bought three puppies from Julian and that both men regarded her with a considerable degree of affection.

'I never mind letting Maud have a puppy,' Julian said. 'I know it'll have a super home even if she is just a teensy-weensy bit inclined to flap.'

Linus recalled Mrs Egremont's having said something about never having bought a puppy which didn't have something go wrong with it, and wondered if that was what he meant. He hadn't himself ever seen signs of her flapping, and said so.

'Oh, she settles down, don't you, Maud, dear? But when she first gets a puppy she imagines everything under the sun is wrong with it. I've told her, she should have faith in her own judgement and her own good management.'

'I always feel puppies are so vulnerable,' she explained.

'They are, but they get more so if you fuss. They're very quick to pick up vibes. I've told you that a hundred times.'

'He's quite right,' Linus said. 'They sense when you're anxious.'

'I know, but I can't help being anxious when I've a new puppy on the premises,' Mrs Egremont said.

Linus had been looking in his catalogue again. 'You've got a lot of dogs entered,' he commented. 'That must put you in with a chance.'

'Sometimes it works against you,' Julian told him. 'If you do well in the lower classes, or in dogs, the judge begins to think "Oh God, I've been putting this man up all along the line, I'd better find someone else," and you don't do so well in the higher classes or in the bitches. Right now I've got some good youngsters, so it's worth the gamble. If I were showing a good mature adult, I'd make sure I had something less good in the lower classes. That way the judge thinks "This dog isn't bad and this poor sod's been down the line in every class, let's put him up and make his day."'

'That's a very cynical view,' Linus said.

'That's *realpolitik*,' Julian replied, grinning.

Linus decided it was time Ted Blandford was included in the conversation. It wasn't so much that the man seemed anything other than perfectly content to let his friend monopolize that end of the proceedings as a feeling that ordinary politeness demanded his inclusion. 'You don't own the dogs in partnership?' he asked.

'We thought about it,' Ted said. 'We decided it would make life too difficult if we split up, especially if the split was acrimonious. Mind you, we cheat on the benching. I ought to be the other end of the line but I always bench my dogs with Julian's and no one up that end's going to complain because it leaves them some empty benches to spill over on to. Works quite well, really.'

'I take it you've met our dear friends, the Chilton-Foliats.' Julian addressed the remark to Linus, lowering his voice as he did so.

'We were introduced, yes,' Linus said.

Julian leant towards them conspiratorially. 'Have you heard the gossip?' he asked.

Linus, who had never heard of the Chilton-Foliats until that day, saw no reason why he should have done, and very little for being interested in it anyway. He said as much, but Mrs Egremont's eyes lit up and, had she been a dog, she would have pricked up her ears quite literally. Instead she had to be content with a metaphorical application of the technique. 'No. What?' she said eagerly.

Ted laughed. 'Don't get excited. It's not nearly as interesting as Julian likes to make out.'

'Ignore him,' Julian ordered. 'Word is—I can't vouch for it, mind you, but the source is impeccable—that he's got a bit on the side *and* they're in a bit of financial bother. I've heard they've put a few bitches out on breeding terms, though they've kept very quiet about *that*.'

'Isn't it quite usual for a bitch to go to someone free, or for very little, in return for puppies back at a later date?' Linus asked.

'Good heavens, yes,' Julian told him. 'Some people do it all the time. The thing is, the Chilton-Foliats have always been rather holier-than-thou about it. *They* don't do that sort of thing. I quote. Always makes those who do sound like the sort of people who steal little old ladies' pension books.'

'From which I deduce that you do sometimes do "things like that",' Linus said drily.

'Oh, sharp, very sharp. You'll have to watch you don't cut yourself.' Julian turned to Mrs Egremont. 'Very bright boy, you've got here. You'd better watch him.'

'If what you heard about the Chilton-Foliats is true, she'd be better off watching them,' Ted interjected. 'They live quite near you, don't they? Don't accept any invitations to tea. You might find they'd decided to solve their financial problems by slipping you a teaspoon of arsenic instead of sugar.'

Mrs Egremont bridled. 'Now you're being as naughty as Julian,' she chided. 'I know you've never liked them but they're not *that* bad. They like to win and they've never learned to lose with a good grace, but that's all.'

'Isn't that enough?' Julian demanded. 'Watch it, that's all I say. Beware of Greeks bearing gifts, and all that. Maybe you'd better employ this veterinary friend of yours as a taster.'

'Now you're just being silly. Besides, they don't live near me. Not near enough for tea invitations, anyway. It's my daughter they live near. I could ask Winifred if she's heard anything,' she said thoughtfully. 'Mind you, I don't even know if they're acquainted with each other. Thetford isn't exactly a village, when all's said and done.'

Linus escorted Mrs Egremont back to her bench and was about to say goodbye and wish her good luck when she dismissed him—temporarily.

'I'll let you have a little wander round on your own now,' she said. 'You don't want to be tied to a little old lady for hours on end.' She glanced at her watch. 'If you come back in about three-quarters of an hour, you ought to be just in time to see Tigger in the ring. You'll like that.'

Seeing Tigger in the ring figured fairly low on Linus's list of things he'd like to do, and strangling old ladies suddenly shot to the top, but then he thought: What the hell? It's only one afternoon and next time I'm at a dog show, I'll make damn sure I don't look her up, so he smiled and said he'd do his best.

He was tempted to go back forthwith to the agricultural part of the show, if not straight home but he didn't because he was still mildly optimistic that he might see just the breed that spoke to his condition.

This was a decision he regretted when he felt a tap on his shoulder and looked round to see Janine Flatford standing behind him.

'Thank goodness I've found you,' she said. 'Maud was getting worried that you hadn't come back so I was detailed to find you. To tell you the truth, I was afraid you might have gone home. They're just.beginning the judging.'

'Haven't you got dogs of your own to get ready?' Linus asked.

She pulled a face. 'Yes, I have and, frankly, that's what I'd rather be doing. But you know Maud. It's much easier to go along with what she wants than to cry off, no matter how valid the reason.'

'She steam-rollers you as well, does she?' Linus said as they threaded their way back to the benches.

'I wouldn't put it quite as strongly as that,' Janine said. 'I feel quite sorry for her: she's an old woman and I don't think she's got many friends. I try to do something about it but I must admit, I'm not at all sorry sometimes that I live in Bedfordshire—too far to be expected to "drop in". Is that too awful of me?'

'It sounds to me like a healthy sense of self-preservation,' Linus told her. 'I like the old biddy but there's no denying she has a talent for . . . for suffocating.'

'That's it exactly—and one does like to breathe from time to time. Still, I do make the effort every so often. I've a couple of tickets for a play at the Key Theatre in Peterborough. I thought I'd ask her if she'd like to come.'

'I'm sure she'd be delighted. What is it? Not too intellectual?'

'Hardly. Just good fun. *Arsenic and Old Lace*. Not exactly the latest, but tried and tested.'

Linus cast his mind back to certain elements of Julian Treorchy's conversation. 'Right up her street,' he said.

Linus had assumed that Mrs Egremont took her showing only semi-seriously; that she was a little old lady who, from

time to time, had a dog with which she had a bit of fun by
entering it at dog shows. Because she was wealthy, she went
to championship shows like this one; had she been hard up
she would probably have contented herself with the sort of
show that had classes for the dog with the waggiest tail or
the dog the judge would most like to take home.

He was wrong. Mrs Egremont might not devote her life
to the showing of dogs, and she might treat her dogs in
what he could only describe as a petsy-wetsy way, but she
showed with deadly professionalism. Linus was no expert
on the handling of dogs for exhibition but he very soon
recognized that a lot of hard work had gone into preparing
Tigger for show. It hadn't been just a matter of bathing
and grooming, but of training. Tigger stood like a rock on
the end of a loose lead, his gaze glued on his owner who
returned the compliment. From time to time Mrs Egremont
glanced towards the judge and ensured that whenever that
lady looked in her direction, Tigger was standing at his
best. Not for Maud Egremont the casual chat with a friend
at the ringside or the exhibitor standing next to her, and
not for Maud Egremont's dog an opportunity to sit down,
roll over, or even drop his tail. While they were in the ring,
they worked. Linus had no idea whether Tigger was a better
Korean Palace Dog than any of the others but if showman-
ship and good handling counted for anything, he deserved
his red card. The blue card for second place went to Meriel
Chilton-Foliat's dog, a stranger was third and Janine Flatford took Reserve. This gave Linus an opportunity to see
what Mrs Egremont had meant about being bad losers. It
wasn't a matter of tearing up the award card or stomping
out of the ring, but whereas the others in the line-up dis-
guised their disappointment to smile and congratulate the
winner before telling their dogs what good boys they'd been,
Mrs Chilton-Foliat's mouth was set in a straight, hard line
as she waited while the judge wrote up her comments on
the winning dogs and when she left the ring, she gave her

dog a quite unnecessarily sharp jerk on the lead to indicate her intention. There was no praise for him.

'Well done,' Linus said as Mrs Egremont ducked under the rope and stood beside him.

'Tigger showed like a real pro, didn't he?' she said proudly.

'So did you,' Linus told her. 'I think the card was won equally by both of you.'

She was obviously pleased, but demurred nevertheless. 'Nonsense. One does all one can to help the dog show himself to best advantage. It's as much about that as about anything else.'

'Congratulations, Maud,' Janine Flatford said as she came out of the ring. 'Tigger looked terrific. You really deserved that.'

It seemed to be Meriel Chilton-Foliat who did all their handling and Linus had the opportunity of seeing her other face when she won a later class. She was willing enough to smile then and had acquired a technique of gracious acceptance of the congratulations of the defeated that was almost patronizing, and Linus felt it spoke volumes for the niceness of the other exhibitors that they hadn't given up congratulating her years ago. She still didn't thank the dog.

Even Linus, who wasn't directly involved, felt the tension in the competition between the hitherto unbeaten dogs for the award of Best of Sex. There were five dogs in contention and the coveted award went to one of Ted Blandford's with the Reserve Best of Sex going to Tigger despite his youth and immaturity. The ringside clapped and so did the handlers of the beaten contenders as the two winners did their lap of honour. Meriel Chilton-Foliat did not join in the applause and, when Mrs Egremont came out of the ring, her comment was not the usual—and deserved—'Well done,' but a commiserating, 'Hard luck, Mrs E. You should have had that.'

Mrs Egremont was having none of that. 'Nonsense.

Tigger's not nearly mature enough yet. We were jolly lucky to do as well as did.'

From the look on her face, Mrs Chilton-Foliat was in total agreement. Linus considered her remark to have been as mean-spirited as possible, in the circumstances, designed to transform pleasure in a win to disgruntlement at not doing better. Both the remark itself and Mrs Egremont's response told him a very great deal about the two ladies, the more so since Mrs Egremont's response was entirely sincere. She wasn't a bad old stick, he thought.

The observation mellowed him and he stayed to keep her company during the rest of the judging despite his lack of interest in the proceedings. Best Bitch went to one of Julian Treorchy's which meant that he and Ted were battling it out for Best of Breed.

'That'll cause a fluttering in the dovecote tonight,' someone said and there was some laughter, none of it malicious. Linus noticed that the Chilton-Foliats didn't join in.

Janine Flatford was standing the other side of them and leaned across to Mrs Egremont. 'Maud,' she said, 'I've got a couple of tickets for *Arsenic and Old Lace* at the Key. Would you like to come with me?'

'What a lovely idea! When is it?'

'Not for a while. Next month. The thirteenth. It's a Thursday.'

Mrs Egremont's face fell and she shook her head. 'How disappointing,' she said. 'Thursday evenings is when I help out at the volunteer shop at the hospital.'

'Couldn't you change it?' Janine Flatford sounded genuinely disappointed.

'I suppose I *could* but that would be an imposition on someone else. If we were talking about some sort of emergency, it would be different, but I can hardly ask them to change it for something as frivolous as a trip to the theatre, can I?'

'I suppose not. I dare say the box office will be able to sell the extra ticket. Another time perhaps.'

As Linus escorted Mrs Egremont back to the benching tent, he said, 'I didn't know you did voluntary work at the hospital.'

She looked surprised. 'Why should you? One doesn't go around waving a banner about it, you know, and the subject never came up.' She grinned. 'My life isn't *exactly* devoted to pleasure.'

He laughed. 'I'm glad to hear it.'

'Now,' she went on, 'there's one more thing you can do for me before you go, if you wouldn't mind.'

'If I can. What is it?'

'Give me a hand with all my paraphernalia back to the car.'

'Gladly, especially if it's that gem I saw in your garage.'

'It is. Here, take this,' and she handed him a folded cage, a folded picnic chair and an imitation leather holdall emblazoned with the words 'Best of Breed' and the name of a well-known brand of dog food. It was quite heavy. She added a similarly adorned towel of excellent quality and execrable design, picked up her handbag and her dog before looking around her and saying, 'That's the lot, I think. Right, follow me.'

Linus did so, and sent up a small prayer of gratitude for the fact that the car park to the dog show was just across the road from the exit. Even though Mrs Egremont's car was parked some way off across the huge field, it was much closer than the park where Linus's car was.

Korean Palace Dogs had been judged late in the day and, since exhibitors could leave when their breed had been finished, by the time Linus and Mrs Egremont crossed into the car park, the cars left were so widely scattered as to justify the thought that it was almost empty. There were in fact probably some two or three hundred cars still left, but, since this represented a tenth of those that had been there by mid-morning, they were very thin on the ground and Linus had no difficulty at all spotting the Armstrong-Siddeley.

'Over there,' he said, nodding because his hands were otherwise occupied.

Mrs Egremont looked back over her shoulder. 'That's right. In line with that big tree and the telegraph pole with the notice on it.'

Linus turned to look back, too. 'So it is. Do you make a careful note when you arrive?'

'Of course I do,' she said scornfully. 'One feels such a fool walking up and down looking for a car and becoming increasingly sure someone's stolen it.'

Actually, Linus thought, it wouldn't be difficult to steal a car towards the end of the day. The place was nearly empty and although there had been a check to ensure no one took out a dog they weren't authorized to remove, there was no similar check at the car park exit. Not all the cars taking dogs to shows were clapped-out estates. There was a higher than average proportion of Volvo estates and Range-Rovers, not to mention all the other four-wheel drive cross-country vehicles that looked the part even if the majority of owners had no real need of such 'tough' vehicles. They would be well worth stealing. So would Mrs Egremont's Armstrong-Siddeley—a collector's piece if ever there was one.

'I hope your car's thief-proof,' he commented as they crossed the field towards it.

'I've locked it, if that's what you mean. I always do.'

'I'd suggest you need something by way of a back-up system. A crook-lock or something. Cheap to buy, simple to fix but too much hassle for a thief to want to risk being seen trying to remove it.'

'Nonsense. They don't want elderly cars like mine. They go for something fast and flash. Getaway cars or tart-carts,' she added incongruously. Linus could only assume she'd

picked the phrase up from a television programme or a
book. He was going to ask her if she knew what it meant
but decided against it: he knew her well enough now to be
able to hazard a shrewd guess that, if she hadn't been able
to guess its meaning when she heard it, she'd ferreted it
out very soon afterwards. She was that sort of woman.

'Your elderly car is probably quite valuable,' he told her.
'They're not often seen these days and it's in very good
condition. You ought to get it valued.'

She shrugged. 'What for? If it's valuable, I don't want
to know: I'd feel obliged to get rid of it and then I'd have
to get used to something else. I *like* that car. It'll see me
out.'

Linus didn't doubt that it would. He saw her dog, her
chattels and herself comfortably disposed and watched her
drive out. Despite her age, she seemed a more than com-
petent driver. Then he went in search of his own car and
very soon found himself wishing he'd taken as much care
as Mrs Egremont to establish his bearings before leaving
it in the first place.

CHAPTER 4

In the weeks that followed his visit to the East of England
Show, Linus gave it no more reflection than is normally
accorded after the event to a pleasant day out. If he thought
about Maud Egremont at all, it was to echo Janine Flatford's gratitude that he lived a long way away from her; to
her dogs and her fellow-exhibitors he gave no thought at
all.

When his telephone went some six weeks later and the
caller identified herself, the name conveyed so little to him
that he was obliged to ask the caller to repeat it.

'Winifred Upperby,' the woman reiterated. 'Maud

Egremont's daughter. We met at my mother's house one afternoon last summer.'

'I remember. You had a husband.'

'I still have. George,' she said tartly. 'You met him, too.'

'Yes, I remember.' This was true enough. He had a clearer mental image of the husband than of the wife. 'What can I do for you?' It sounded marginally less rude than 'What do you want?' which was what he meant.

'Nothing. I'm ringing on behalf of my mother, though why on earth she can't pick up the phone and ring you herself, goodness only knows.'

Linus's spirits, which had been quite high because it was a glorious autumn day, sank. He had escaped Mrs Egremont's hederatic instincts and had no desire to be within their reach again. 'If she needs a vet,' he said, 'tell her to go to her usual one. It would be quite unethical for me to treat anything.'

'It's nothing to do with that. Nothing to do with those horrid little dogs, either, except indirectly. It's your company she wants.' There was a brief pause during which Linus quickly reviewed the range of get-out options he could muster at short notice. 'At a funeral,' Winifred concluded.

'A *funeral*?' Linus was incredulous. Why a funeral? What funeral? A thought struck him. Mrs Egremont was a somewhat quirky old woman. Could she have died and written something in her will insisting on his presence at her funeral for some reason known only to her? He wouldn't put it past her. But if that were so, Winifred would hardly have expressed surprise that her mother wasn't prepared to telephone him herself. 'Whose funeral?' he asked.

'A friend of Mummy's. She says you knew her. Flatford. Janine Flatford. Mummy had had a dog or two from her, I believe. It was certainly through dogs that she knew her.'

'I remember her. Nice woman.'

'So I believe. Almost normal, by all accounts. Not at all like the majority of these dog breeders.'

Linus cast his mind back to the show. Janine Flatford—he had no idea whether she was Mrs, Miss or the revolting Americanism, Ms—had seemed perfectly healthy and far too young for anyone to assume the imminence of death. 'Was it expected? I mean, it must have been a heart attack or something. Was there a history?'

'I've no information about Ms Flatford's medical state,' Winifred said so acidly that Linus decided her use of the hated 'Ms' was probably intended to indicate nothing more than her disapproval of the woman and everything connected with her, despite her earlier qualification. 'I shouldn't think it contributed anything towards her death, however. I gather she was murdered.'

'Murdered? You mean someone killed her?'

'Isn't that what most people mean when they use the word?'

'Yes, but . . .' Linus groped his way backwards towards the arm of the sofa and perched there. Murder is like road accidents: something one reads about every day, something one knows happens but something which only ever happens to other people, to people one doesn't know, a completely irrational belief which makes the reality even more difficult to come to terms with when it happens.

'What happened?' he asked.

Winifred was briskly matter-of-fact. 'It appears she went to the theatre in Peterborough. Do you know the theatre there?'

'No.'

'It's quite a small one but in a lovely setting on the river bank. The city fathers have had the whole of the river bank landscaped and laid out as a park—the sort that looks natural but isn't—and you can stroll quite a long way along its course if you want to. It's quite a popular place for the audience to go to get fresh air during the interval.'

'It would be. A bit like Glyndebourne, I imagine.'

'Yes, quite.' She sounded taken aback, as if a common-or-garden vet would not have been expected to draw that comparison. 'It seems Janine Flatford went for a stroll afterwards. Rather foolish, really. During the interval there would have been plenty of other people about but afterwards it must have been virtually deserted, and one hears such things these days . . . Anyway, be that as it may, that's what she did. She was attacked, beaten up and her body thrown into the river, though I'm not quite sure whether she was already dead by that time or just too far gone to do anything about it. Her handbag was missing, I gather, so the general feeling is that she was mugged. They seem to think she put up a fight and that's why she was killed. Wouldn't you think any woman would have the intelligence to hand over her handbag in the reasonable expectation that the mugger would then run off?'

'It would certainly seem a more sensible thing to do,' Linus agreed. 'I can't quite see where I come in all this. I can understand your mother's wanting to go to the funeral, but why with me?'

'How should I know?' Winifred snapped. 'I long since abandoned any attempt to make rhyme or reason out of her idiosyncrasies.'

Linus wasn't at all sure he liked being described as an idiosyncrasy, and it showed in his tone. 'She must have given some explanation,' he said.

'Oh, she did, though what that had to do with the price of fish, goodness only knows. She says she feels responsible for the woman's death—indirectly, of course. Even Mummy isn't silly enough to confess to murder. It seems this Flatford woman had originally had two tickets for the play in question and had asked Mummy if she'd like to go with her and Mummy turned it down because it was her evening at the hospital. She now says she could have asked someone to swop with her and didn't because it always causes resentment and bad feelings but that if she had, she would have been with her friend and the attack would probably never have happened. So she feels guilty.'

'I can understand that,' Linus said. 'Has it been pointed out to her that, if there was more than one assailant, there might well have been two women in the river?'

'George and I did make that point.'

'Or that your mother might have decided she was too tired for a post-theatre stroll and gone home, leaving her friend in exactly the same position? If that had happened, she'd feel even worse.'

'Those possibilities have been mentioned, too.'

'I still don't see where I come in.'

'Apparently you knew all about this theatre visit, though what that has to do with it, I can't imagine. I suppose she thinks you'll be more sympathetic than we are.'

Which, Linus thought, wouldn't be too difficult if her tone was anything to go by. 'When is it?' he asked, preparing the way for discovering some immovable obstacle to his attending.

'Tomorrow afternoon at three o'clock in Bedford, but Mummy wants you to go over to Hunstanton and pick her up. I've already told her that's an unreasonable burden to put on you. I've also told her that as a civil servant you won't be able to get away at such short notice.'

She was offering him excuses with a quite unwonted generosity of spirit. Not for the first time, Linus noted just how much a voice gave away over the telephone, where it was disembodied and there were no visual signals to distract or deceive. He formed the distinct impression that Winifred Upperby was very anxious he should be unable to attend. He wondered why.

'It certainly wouldn't be easy,' he replied cautiously.

'Exactly,' she said enthusiastically. 'It isn't even as if you lived in this area. Why, you'd have to travel right across England and then half way back to get to the church and then repeat it all in reverse afterwards. It's a ridiculous request. In any case, George and I have told her we'll be only too happy to take her ourselves. She says she'll have none of it, but, since you won't be able to make it, she'll have to make do with her family.'

Linus hadn't the slightest inclination to attend the funeral of a woman with whom he was barely acquainted in the company of another he found demanding on a day which would entail, at a conservative estimate, some nine or ten hours of driving. For those reasons alone, he was perfectly willing to plead pressure of work, staff shortages and urgent appointments. The fact that he didn't was due entirely to Winifred's overplaying her hand. She had said too much. He was quite sure, not only that the Upperbys weren't the least happy at the prospect of ferrying Mrs Egremont to a funeral in Bedford themselves, but also that, if the old lady hadn't insisted she wanted him, they wouldn't even have suggested doing so and would have found it impossible if the suggestion had emanated from Mrs Egremont in the first place. He hadn't the slightest idea why they should be so opposed to his attendance but it seemed to him that that very opposition was the best possible reason for his making the effort. No doubt he would regret it, especially since he could think of any number of more enjoyable ways of passing the time—not least among them, work—but that was a sacrifice he was willing to make out of sheer, unadulterated bloody-mindedness.

'No, it won't be easy,' he said, 'but I can imagine how upset your mother is and to refuse to take her would be very selfish as well as unnecessarily unkind. I'll sort something out. I should be able to get to her by, say, one o'clock. Will you let her know that for me?'

He could perfectly well telephone her himself but felt it would be more politic to leave it to Winifred. Besides, he didn't want to have to listen to a long and possibly emotional reprise of what the daughter had already told him.

'You can do it? Are you sure? I mean, you're not putting yourself out or anything?'

'No more than I'm prepared to,' he replied.

'Well, it's really very kind of you. George and I are most grateful to you. Most grateful.'

Linus wondered if the repetition was supposed to erase the insincerity. They might be grateful not to have to go themselves but he doubted very much that they were glad to see him so willing to take their place. 'Think nothing of it,' he said. 'What are friends for?'

'I'll warn Mummy to expect you.'

Linus put the phone down and cursed himself. What had he let himself in for? And why was he stupid enough to land himself in something he wanted to avoid just to spike the guns of someone he didn't much like—and, when all was said and done, someone he didn't much like on a basis of nothing more than a feeling, an impression.

The funeral was very well attended and Linus recognized a number of those present as being people he had seen at the show, to not all of whom he had been introduced. It was a small relief to be able to make desultory conversation at the wake with people who weren't total strangers. Ted and Julian were there, both obviously having attended out of genuine respect for the dead woman. Meriel Chilton-Foliat was worried about Janine's dogs.

'Do you know what's going to happen to them?' she asked Mrs Egremont.

'I don't, but I can't believe Janine didn't make some sort of provision,' she replied.

'She had so many really good ones,' Meriel went on. 'It would be such a pity if they were lost to the breed.'

'Meriel was all for offering to take them,' her husband butted in, 'but I had to put my foot down. She got fed up with being a housewife and decided to go back to being a career-woman, and I pointed out to her that she just wouldn't have been able to take on the extra responsibility.'

'What are you doing?' Linus asked, more for the sake of finding something to say than out of any great desire to know.

Meriel seemed flustered. 'It's just a toe in the water at the moment,' she said. 'I'm only working afternoons for the time being. See how it goes, and all that.'

'It's a little PR job in a section of the cultural heritage industry,' Charles said. 'Meriel's very good at getting ideas across. I'd rather she stayed at home, of course, but if this is what she really wants to do, far be it from me to stand in the way. It would take a brave man these days to stop his wife picking up the reins of her career again. Mrs Egremont's daughter didn't bring her today?' he went on.

'No,' Linus said. 'I gather she and her husband offered but Mrs Egremont said she wanted me. So here I am.'

'Very noble,' Charles commented and Linus wasn't sure whether or not he was being sarcastic. 'Tell me, did you get the chance to drive that car?'

Linus smiled. 'It was offered—and I'd be lying if I said I wasn't tempted, but this is a long way and I wanted to be reasonably sure we'd not only get here but get back as well, and I'm not quite sure how well that car has been maintained in the purely mechanical sense.'

'No expense spared, I think,' Charles told him. 'It gets her to shows all over the country. You'd probably have been all right.'

'I expect you're right,' Linus told him. 'What do you drive yourself?'

Charles made a deprecating gesture. 'Volvo Estate—like a lot of dog breeders. Mind you, it's a bit past its sell-by date now. I had hoped to trade it in this year but what with the recession and all that . . .' His voice tailed off, implying no further explanation was necessary.

Linus nodded. 'One of the advantages of being a civil

servant,' he said. 'Not much danger of losing your job. Makes up for the pay.'

'I can imagine.' It wasn't a concept that appeared to give him much pleasure.

Then Linus spotted another familiar face, one which looked far more ill-at-ease than the others and, since he had always felt rather sorry for Sharon Dedham, he made his excuses to Charles and Meriel and went across to speak to her.

'I don't suppose you remember me,' he said. 'I came with Mrs Egremont when she bought a puppy from you.'

Sharon smiled and her unhealthily pasty face came close to lighting up. 'I remember you all right,' she replied. 'You were very flattering about my puppies. That meant a lot to me. People think if you live in a council house and don't have many dogs that what you do have can't be up to much and you won't be able to look after them properly.'

'It's not an environment I'd ever recommend to anyone taking up the hobby,' Linus said. 'You seem to have overcome the problems though, and Mrs Egremont's doing very well with Tigger.'

'Yes. I'm glad. We haven't been able to get to the shows this year—Kevin lost his job, you see—so I've been very glad to have my affix in the ring and winning, even if it is with someone else on the other end of the lead.'

'Your husband hasn't come with you?'

'No. He didn't want me to come. Said Janine was the cause of all our troubles and he didn't see why we should spend any more time or money on her now she was dead and of no conceivable future use to us. He got quite nasty about it. But I liked Janine. She was good to me, so I decided that this time I'd do what *I* wanted and not what I was told.'

'Good for you,' Linus said, and as he spoke, he noticed for the first time that there was a contusion on her cheekbone that was almost, but not entirely, hidden by a neatly combed fold of lank, mousy hair. 'Are you all right?' he asked.

The direction of his gaze must have explained the question, for she put up a hand to smooth the hair down more firmly over the cheekbone. 'This?' she said. 'It's nothing. I bumped into the bedroom door.'

It was hardly the most original explanation but it wasn't Linus's job to press for a better one. 'You should take more water with it,' he said, equally unoriginally.

Sharon managed a smile. 'That's what Kevin said.'

'I know it's none of my business,' Linus went on, 'but what did your husband mean when he said Janine Flatford was the cause of all your troubles?'

'It was a silly thing to say—and quite untrue. He was as keen as I was at the time. I bought our first KPD from her, you see. He let me because he thought it was going to make our fortunes—or at least give us a bit in the bank— only it didn't work out quite like that.'

'It seldom does,' Linus said. 'It's just about the worst possible reason for buying a dog.'

'I did try to make that clear to him at the time but he didn't want to listen and since I'd always wanted a KPD ever since I was a child, I didn't push it too hard. I wasn't to know he'd be out of work within a few years.'

'Will you be able to keep them?'

'I'm determined to, no matter what. Mind you, I wouldn't say so to Kevin but he's right about one thing.'

'What's that?'

She glanced rather nervously about. 'It's a horrid thing even to think, but sometimes you can't help what you think and Mrs Egremont's very old. The story in the breed is that when she dies, her dogs go back to their breeders with a lot of money for their support. I don't even know if the story's true, but you can imagine what Kevin's been thinking.'

Linus could, all too clearly. 'Let's just hope it's an idea

he doesn't follow up,' he said, trying to make it sound like a light-hearted remark.

She chuckled with genuine amusement. 'Oh, dear, I'm sure one shouldn't laugh at a funeral, but Kevin isn't like that. He's got a temper and it sometimes gets the better of him. Quite often, in fact,' she amended, 'but he wouldn't do anything *really* nasty.'

Linus privately thought that GBH, not to mention wife-beating, were nasty enough to be going on with but he saw no good reason for saying so and decided instead that it was time he made his way back to Mrs Egremont and persuaded her to leave. There was a long journey to Norfolk ahead of them and then he had to drive all the way back to Oxford—and she was bound to expect him to stay for a cup of tea at the very least.

As they walked back down the road to where Linus had parked his car, they passed a none-too-new Volvo estate with its bonnet up and Meriel Chilton-Foliat tapping a well-shod but impatient foot on the pavement. The car was maroon, Linus noticed with satisfaction.

'Problem?' he asked.

Charles's head emerged. 'Nothing I can't fix—unless you're a good mechanic as well as a vet.'

'Me? Good God, no. I know where to put the petrol and oil and I can recognize a fan-belt, but that's about it. I'm quite at home with the innards of a cow, but the viscera of the internal combustion engine are a complete mystery to me.'

'Charles is really rather good with cars,' his wife said. 'Does all his own maintenance.'

Charles Chilton-Foliat stood up. 'Not well enough, it seems,' he said wryly. 'It's a bit of a hobby of mine but I'm strictly amateur. In this case, though, I think the alternator's gone. We'd better go back inside and ask if we can borrow the Yellow Pages to find a dealer.'

'I'm impressed,' Linus said, sincerely. 'You'll want to be

getting on with it so we won't keep you chatting. See you some time.'

'At another show, perhaps.'

'Perhaps.' Linus didn't think it was very likely.

'Funny couple,' he said when they were back in his car and negotiating their way through Bedford.

'Meriel and Charles? They're all right, really. Charles always reminds me a bit of George: same aspirations but more taste and less money.'

'He was saying something which sounded as if the recession has hit him quite hard.'

'Must be very hard if Charles Chilton-Foliat's prepared to admit it. That's probably the real reason his wife's taken a part-time job.'

Linus thought it more than likely. 'What line was she in? Advertising? Journalism?'

Mrs Egremont frowned. 'Shouldn't think so. I don't think she's quite that well endowed up top. No, come to think of it, I've a vague recollection something was said about her having been Charles's secretary—and he's one of these people who puts "Company Director" when he has to fill in his job, and that covers a multitude of sins. What made you think advertising?'

'He said something about her job being PR in—what did he call it?—the cultural heritage industry.'

Mrs Egremont laughed. 'That means she sells cloakroom tickets at the Tower of London.'

There was an aptness in the comment. 'Too far to cycle to work,' he said.

'Did I see you talking to Sharon Dedham?' Mrs Egremont asked after they had driven the next mile or two in silence.

'Yes. Difficult. I gather she came against that awful husband's wishes. It looked as if he'd clouted her.'

'Wouldn't surprise me if he had. Now there really *is* a nasty piece of work. She's such a nice girl, too. Or at least,

she would be if she didn't have him breathing down her
neck.'

Linus hesitated, uncertain to what extent to mention
what was in his mind. 'Did you know your plans for your
dogs after you die are fairly widely known?'

'I've never kept it a close secret.'

Linus said nothing.

'Let me guess,' Mrs Egremont went on. 'Kevin Dedham
has heard about it and has speculated on ways of turning
it to immediate advantage.'

'It would appear so,' Linus said cautiously. 'Something
like that, anyway.'

'That's all right, then. He won't do anything about it.'

Linus laughed. 'I don't suppose he will but I can't say
I'd be quite so positive about it as you are.'

'Kevin's a lot of things, most of them not at all nice,'
Mrs Egremont said. 'However, he isn't silly. He's certainly
not daft enough to mention the idea to anyone—not even
Sharon—if that was really in his mind. No, it's just Kevin's
choice of daydream.'

'Charming,' Linus commented but, upon reflection, he
decided his companion was probably right.

Linus hadn't been aware of the presence of anyone at the
funeral, either in the church or at the graveside, who
couldn't have been ranked as a mourner. There were two
likely reasons for this. One was that he hadn't known more
than a handful of those attending, anyway. The other was
that it hadn't occurred to him to be on the lookout for such
people. He was therefore totally unprepared for a visit from
the police.

'Detective-Inspector Rievaulx, of the Cambridgeshire
Constabulary,' the foremost of the two men on his doorstep
introduced himself, holding up his warrant-card. 'And this
is Detective-Sergeant Chacombe. May we come in?'

Linus opened the door wider. 'I suppose you may,' he

said, standing aside. 'I take it this has to do with the death of Janine Flatford.'

'Now why should you assume that?' the Inspector asked.

'It doesn't take a master of deduction to reach that conclusion,' Linus told him. 'She's the only person with whom I've had the slightest contact who has died in the sort of circumstances that would warrant your appearance on the scene, and I've not been up to anything illegal on your bailiwick.'

'Not even parking on a double yellow line?' the Inspector asked drily.

'Especially not parking on a double yellow line,' Linus said firmly. 'You have to be a diplomat or a millionaire these days to play that game and I'm neither.'

'How well did you know Mrs Flatford?'

It was the first time Linus had heard her status mentioned. He was sure he'd never heard mention of a husband. 'Not well at all—very superficially, in fact. I'd only ever met her the once, at this year's East of England Show.'

'But you went to her funeral?'

'Yes.'

'Tell me, Mr Rintoul, why should you go all the way to Bedford for the funeral of a woman you scarcely knew?'

'In the normal course of events, I wouldn't have. In fact, in the normal course of events I wouldn't even have known she was dead. And just to ensure that your record is absolutely accurate, I should perhaps make it clear that I didn't go from Oxford to Bedford to attend the funeral. I went from Oxford to Hunstanton to Bedford—and then did the same journey in reverse afterwards.'

'And why would you have done that?'

'To take one of the other mourners. A Mrs Egremont. Maud Egremont.'

'Ah, yes—Mrs Egremont. A remarkable old lady, don't you think?'

Linus smiled with a noticeable lack of humour. 'Then
you know why I went to the funeral.'

'I know why other people *said* you went. That may not
be the same thing.'

'I very much doubt if there's much divergence.'

'You'd be surprised by how much accounts can diverge.
Let's have your version.'

Briefly, Linus told him about Winifred's phone call.

'Didn't you think it was an imposition?'

'Yes. I was initially disinclined to go. I changed my
mind.'

'Evidently. Why?'

'Mrs Egremont's daughter put my back up. It was quite
obvious she didn't want me to go and she was handing me
my excuses on a plate. I can dream up my own excuses.
So I said I'd go.'

'Just to spite Mrs Upperby?'

'Well, yes, I suppose that's what it amounts to. Rather
petty, put like that.'

'What made you think she didn't want you to go?'

'It's difficult to say, precisely,' Linus said, after considering the matter. 'It was partly that she was so keen to give me
excuses, but that wasn't the whole story. The telephone's a
funny thing, Inspector: I'm sure you've noticed how voices
give so much more away when there's no visual image to
distract you.'

The Inspector was not going to be led into commenting
on that and remained silent, but it was an expectant silence.

'Just had the very clear impression that she hadn't
wanted to ring me in the first place and wanted nothing so
much as to be able to convey my refusal to her mother,'
Linus concluded.

'And you naturally wouldn't wish to upset Mrs Egremont,' the Inspector commented.

'I gathered from Mrs Upperby that she was already very
upset. I wouldn't have wanted to add to her distress but if

I'm honest, I'd have to admit that a desire not to upset her wasn't at the forefront of my thoughts.'

'So let's get back to Mrs Flatford. What do you know about her death?'

'Only what Mrs Upperby told me: that she was mugged, her handbag stolen, and her body thrown in the river. She'd been to see *Arsenic and Old Lace* at the Key, which I gather is on the river-side.'

Inspector Rievaulx flipped back through his notebook in silence and re-read something he'd written down previously. 'Mrs Upperby told you all those details?'

'Yes. I think she said that there was a question whether Mrs Flatford had actually been dead when she was thrown in.'

'But she told you the name of the theatre and what she'd been to see?'

Linus cast his mind back. How much of that detail had Winifred passed on? 'She may not have—I may have assumed that. I can't remember the conversation verbatim.'

'Can you tell me why you should assume that was the play she'd seen?'

'I knew she was going to it.'

'And yet you'd only met her once, nearly a month before her death?'

'That's right. It was at the show. She told Mrs Egremont she had two tickets for it and would she like to come. Mrs Egremont said she couldn't because Thursday was her evening at the hospital, and when Janine Flatford had been killed, Mrs Egremont felt very guilty about it because she thought that if only she'd gone with her, Mrs Flatford would still have been alive.'

'Mrs Egremont told you this?'

'No, her daughter did. The mother didn't refer to it.'

'So, since you knew which play and which day of the

week, you could easily have been there, too. You might even have offered to use the other seat.'

'I suppose I could, but it never crossed my mind—and nor did murder. I'm not a violent man, Inspector, and although civil servants in the provinces aren't among the highest paid mortals in the land, I've certainly no need to resort to mugging for a bit of cash.'

'Where were you on the evening of the Thursday in question, Mr Rintoul?'

'By a quirk of Fate, I wasn't, thank God, sitting at home watching television or listening to the radio—which is what I do more evenings than not,' Linus said, relieved. 'My son's decided to get engaged so I took him and his fiancée out for a celebratory dinner. Do you want their names and addresses?'

'We'd rather have that of the restaurant. I take it you'd booked in advance so there will be a record?'

'Have you ever tried to get into the Elizabeth on a Thursday night without a reservation, Inspector?' Linus demanded.

'One of those, is it? I'm not conversant with Oxford's eating-places. It is in the city, I take it?'

'Just across the road from St Aldate's police station.'

'Very convenient. Do you remember when you got there and when you left?'

'I'd booked a table for eight but we were a little late. Eight-fifteen, at a guess, but certainly no later than half past, and I was home by half past eleven. I saw the other two into a taxi and then got one for myself. I suppose we left about eleven.'

'And you were there all evening?'

'Of course I was—and even if I hadn't been, I'd hardly have been able to drive all the way to Peterborough, murder someone and then drive all the way back, would I?'

The Sergeant grinned. 'Your absence would certainly have been noted, sir,' he said.

Inspector Rievaulx stood up. 'Thank you for your cooperation, Mr Rintoul. We shall check this out, of course, but I've no doubt we shall be able to eliminate you from our inquiries. We have to look into everyone, you understand.'

'Working on the old assumption that the murderer returns to the scene of the crime—or, in this case, to his victim's funeral, I suppose,' Linus said, leading the way to the front door.

'You'd be surprised how often it pays off,' the Inspector said. 'To say nothing of all the other things one learns along the way. Good afternoon, Mr Rintoul.'

'Goodbye,' Linus replied.

CHAPTER 5

The visit of the police annoyed Linus rather than worried him. He knew they were only doing their job and that following up those who attended the funeral without having any obvious connection with the deceased was a routine part of their duty. He knew he had nothing to worry about. Quite apart from the fact that he hadn't killed Janine Flatford—which these days was no justification for peace of mind—he had a cast-iron alibi: the restaurant would know he had taken up his reservation, his signature was on the cheque and even though they might not be able to swear that he had been at the table all evening, it would have been logistically impossible to have got to Peterborough and back. He thought there was a good chance the restaurant staff would remember him: he wasn't a particularly vain man, but he did pride himself on his neatly trimmed, George V beard which served two purposes—it hid some of his scarred face and gave it a distinction of a more complimentary sort; he had, in fact, originally grown it under his wife's direction because, she said, it made his quite ordinary face look 'distinguished'. He had retained it despite the fact that he had to suffer the occasional nudge-nudge and the suggestion that he might be a by-blow of, variously, the late monarch's father, the late Tsar or the late Kaiser. There was something about that particular kind of beard that made all men with one look like kinsmen. All the same, he had an affection for it and it did mean the restaurant would be likely to remember him.

The annoyance was due to his having been dragged into something unpleasant against his will. Not that he was ever any more willing than the next man to be dragged into something unpleasant, but it did mean that Mrs Egremont might be more difficult to unclamp than he had thought. She was a remarkable old lady by any standards, and a very kind-hearted one, too, but she also had a streak of quite ruthless selfishness which was certainly proof against hints and would probably ride rough-shod over more par-ticularly expressed objections. No, that was unfair, he amended, gazing out of the office window at the singularly uninspiring view of yet another 'temporary' prefabricated wing of Government Buildings, she wouldn't use rough shoes so much as emotional blackmail. It would be quite subtly exerted, but emotional blackmail was what it would be.

He had decided to immerse himself in work because he had learnt long ago that it was a pretty effective dissipator of annoyance, frustration and sporadic, non-debilitating depression. Clearing a backlog of paperwork was a particu-larly efficacious employment because it precluded the mind's wandering on to any other topic and its end result was a justifiable pride in seeing the in-tray empty and the files neatly stashed away. Linus could usually depend upon there being a backlog to work on because in the normal course of events he hated paperwork and systematically worked to the principle that if a thing was worth doing, it was worth delaying. He infinitely preferred visiting cattle-markets and farms but this more congenial activity invariably involved journeys that were long enough for his mind to have free rein. Paperwork was nothing but a chore imposed by a bureaucracy that wouldn't know a Limousin from a Light Sussex—though he was prepared to concede, grudgingly, that even a London-based MAFF clerk might know a cow from a chicken if each resembled the drawings in a children's book—but even chores could be turned to good account.

Len Trevarrick came in and perched on the edge of Linus's desk. 'Not often we get you in here for more than quarter of an hour at a time,' he said, without animosity.

Linus was prepared to think of Len as his boss because, as Divisional Veterinary Officer, that's what he was. He could not bring himself to think of him—much less refer to him—as his superior. It was a bit like his occasional encounters with the aristocracy who owned much of the agricultural land in the area. More often than not a mere veterinary officer dealt only with the farm manager but occasionally the owner would be there and, while Linus could bring himself to address them as Lord This or Lady That before reverting to 'you', he could never bring himself to utter the dire words 'my lord' or 'my lady', and never ceased to marvel that farm managers—educated graduates these days, not forelock-tugging peasants—seemed to have no such qualms.

'Guilty conscience,' Linus told him. 'I thought of it all piling up and it kept me awake so I thought I'd better come in and do something about it.'

'Is that so?' Trevarrick said that with studied politeness that implies total disbelief. 'Thought maybe you were having woman-trouble.'

Linus laughed. 'You weren't far out, though not in the way you meant.'

'So you're still seeing Madeleine?'

'Who? Oh, Madeleine.' Linus was slightly shocked to

discover that he had almost forgotten all about her. So much for true love. 'No, that's over, but it's nothing to do with her. Why? Does it matter?'

'No. It's just that if she's still an item, she's included, but any current girlfriend will do just as well.'

'Just as well for what?'

'Our Silver Wedding. Would you believe we've stuck it out for twenty-five years?'

'Are you after congratulations or commiserations?' Linus asked.

'Prezzies, I'm afraid. The wife's decided to hold some sort of bash. "Leave it to me," she said. "I'll do all the arranging. All you'll have to do is sign the cheques." Just the sort of arrangement every sane man dreads. Anyway, we'd like you to come and if you've got a current girlfriend, she's welcome too.'

'Unlikely, I think,' Linus told him, 'but I'd love to come. When is it?'

Trevarrick told him the date and venue. 'Though I says it as shouldn't, the wife's actually rather good at this sort of thing—I wouldn't let her know that, mind you,' he added hastily.

'Don't suppose you need to,' Linus said. 'Wives usually have a pretty shrewd idea of where their talents lie. Are Silver Weddings like the original in having shopping-lists?'

'Apparently not. I gather it's assumed the happy couple have all the necessities so it's left to the guests' discretion. At least we won't get ten toasters.'

'No, you'll be stuck with twenty-five silver-plated things to hold after-dinner mints. I think they're called gondolas.'

Trevarrick blanched. 'They're not even useful. I hope you're joking.'

'More importantly, they're usually very badly designed,' Linus told him. 'I'll find something else. Got a napkin-ring, have you?'

'You're a sarcastic bastard,' Trevarrick said affably.

'You'll get a proper printed thing in due course—all wedding-bells and silver ribbons, I expect. You'll love that.'

'I promise it pride of place on the mantelpiece,' Linus said. 'Let's face it, there's not many these days who stick it out that long. Silver Weddings are becoming an endangered species. Now will you go away and leave me to it?'

Linus looked at the man on the doorstep and frowned. They had met before—he was sure of that—but he couldn't quite place him. The penny dropped a split second before the man introduced himself.

'I'm George Upperby,' he said. 'We met at Maud Egremont's. I'm her son-in-law.'

'Husband of Winifred,' Linus said. 'Come in. How is Mrs Egremont? I hope she's in good health. Or does this visit mean she's not?'

It was George Upperby's turn to frown. 'She's as well as can be expected,' he said cautiously. 'She's had a chest infection which she doesn't seem to be able to throw off, but then, I expect you knew that.'

Linus gestured an invitation to sit down. 'Tea? Coffee? Something stronger?'

'Coffee, thank you. I'm driving.'

Linus went through into the kitchen to put the kettle on. 'I'm sorry to hear she's been unwell and, no, I didn't know it. Why should you think I did?'

'I assumed you were in contact with her. Letters, phone calls, that sort of thing.'

'She wants to keep in touch. I interpret that as Christmas cards.'

'But you took her to the Flatford woman's funeral. That rates a bit higher than Christmas cards.'

'At your mother-in-law's specific request—as you are very well aware.'

'You could have refused.'

Linus brought the coffee in, having put the biscuits back

in the tin. It didn't look as if Upperby's visit was particularly friendly in intention though its purpose was still unexplained, and Linus saw no reason to waste good digestives on him. 'Yes, I could, and if you want to know the truth, I very nearly did. Do you know why I didn't?'

'No idea.'

'Sheer bloody-mindedness.'

'I don't follow.'

'No? It's quite simple. Your wife was so keen to suggest all the reasons I might give for crying off that it was clear she—or perhaps both of you—didn't want me to go. I wondered why. So I went.'

'And were you any the wiser?'

'No, as a matter of fact.' Linus studied the self-satisfied face opposite. 'What's the reason for this visit?' he asked. 'You weren't just passing by and decided to drop in, and the sort of questions you've been asking go a little beyond the social niceties one expects from unannounced visits by people with whom one is barely acquainted.'

'It isn't a social call,' George Upperby said shortly. 'And I wouldn't have come if I didn't think it was important. Winifred is very worried.'

'About her mother?'

'Indirectly, yes.'

'And she thinks I can help?'

Upperby barked a short laugh. 'You could put it like that.'

'Perhaps you'd stop being cryptic and come to the point,' Linus said sharply. 'I wasn't expecting you and I've quite a lot to do today so, if you'd state your business and be gone, I'd be more than grateful.'

'It's quite simple. Keep away from Winifred's mother.'

Linus regarded his visitor steadily. 'Keep away from Mrs Egremont,' he repeated. 'Do I infer from this that you'd like me to emigrate?'

His visitor looked taken aback. 'I wasn't thinking in quite

such drastic terms but I must say, there couldn't be a better solution.'

Sarcasm being obviously wasted on George Upperby, Linus thought he'd better clarify. 'It's a bit difficult to see how I can keep any further away from her without moving abroad. I don't exactly live on her doorstep and I haven't seen her since that funeral.'

'I don't think that's altogether true,' Upperby said.

'What you choose to think is your own business,' Linus told him. 'It doesn't alter the facts.'

'It's certainly not what I hear,' George Upperby went on. 'The general feeling is that you've been dancing attendance on her for quite some time.'

'Then the general feeling—whatever that's supposed to mean—is way out. Good God, man, you make it sound as if I were some sort of gigolo! Mrs Egremont is old enough to be my mother.'

'She herself refers to you as her toy-boy.'

'I know she does. She thinks it's funny. It isn't a joke I share but I suspect that the more I protest about it, the more she'll use the expression. Your mother-in-law is a very determined old lady, and she can be a very wearing one.'

'She's rich, too. Very rich.'

'I'd noticed.'

'I'll bet you have.'

'Don't come the heavy irony with me, Upperby,' Linus said, angry now. 'If you've got some hare-brained notion that I'm "dancing attendance" on your mother-in-law in order to part her from some of her cash, you're way off-beam.'

'Oh, I think you're far too clever to play that game—and in any case, she'd spot it. She's no fool. No, you're playing a waiting game.'

'Am I, now? And what sort of game would that be?'

'You're insinuating yourself into her good graces in anticipation of being left very well off when she's dead.'

Linus's amusement was unfeigned. 'You really are way off-beam,' he said. 'Do you expect me to believe you don't know what the provisions of her will are? I'm afraid that won't wash—she told me herself that she had told you. She also told me you weren't very happy about it. She reckoned you were well enough off not to need more. I did tell her the well-off rarely saw it that way, but she felt the dogs were more important. The estate's to be divided between the people who bred her dogs, though I'm not sure what happens to the ones she had from Mrs Flatford now that their breeder's dead.'

George Upperby snorted. 'You'll be telling me next that you didn't know she'd changed her will or what the new provisions are,' he said.

'That's exactly what I'm telling you.'

'Your influence is evident right through it.'

'You'd better explain.'

'At least she's stopped short of leaving it all to you, but whether the dog breeders are going to be happy to have you deciding what they get and checking up on them all along the line remains to be seen.'

Linus groaned. 'I told her she should make provision to check the dogs weren't put down as soon as the breeders had the money in their little hot hands—and I was adamant that I didn't want the job of checking.'

'Not adamant enough,' Upperby said in a tone that implied Linus didn't mean a word of it. 'It's bad enough for Winifred to have to stand by and see all that her father put together wasted on a handful of dogs and some feckless dog breeders, without finding a complete stranger has come along and wormed his way into gaining control, and I won't stand by and see my wife hurt like this.'

Linus's face was rigid with anger. With great self-control, he relieved his visitor of his coffee-cup and placed it back on the tray. 'You've outstayed what little welcome you had,' he said. 'Now leave. You needn't bother to come back.'

'I'll go when I have your assurance that you'll keep right away from my mother-in-law,' Upperby said, getting to his feet not because he had any intention of leaving yet but because he was otherwise at a psychological disadvantage with Linus standing over him.

'There's only one assurance I'm prepared to give you,' Linus said, 'and that's that if you don't get out of my house this instant, I'll call the police and have you thrown out.'

George Upperby sneered. 'I don't think you'll involve them,' he said.

'Believe me, I mean it. Out!'

There was something in Linus's tone that made his visitor edge towards the door but he wasn't going just yet. 'I'm warning you, Rintoul. If I catch wind of you sniffing round my mother-in-law again, I'll make damned sure you regret it.'

'Grow up, Upperby. This isn't some second-rate film any more than it's Sicily or the Italian quarter of New York. I shall do what I've always done, which is exactly what I want to do. If it makes you happy, your comments—wishes, threats, call them what you will—are duly noted. I don't suppose you're interested in my advice, but, for what it's worth, I suggest you tread very carefully indeed because you've just uttered a threat—a nicely nebulous one, admittedly, but a threat none the less—so if anything untowards befalls me, your name is bound to crop up. Isn't it?'

The front door was open by this time and Upperby was going back to his expensive and uninteresting car. It would have been difficult to decide which of the two men was the more angry: Linus at the imputation regarding his motives or Upperby at the failure of his mission. He was not accustomed to people less well-heeled than himself being quite so defiant, nor did he like being manipulated. He couldn't quite work out how Linus had been able to get him out of the house before he had been able to implement his second strategy which would have involved his cheque-book.

Maud Egremont's previous will had been such as to make
contesting it a relatively simple matter of painting a picture
of a little old lady who was so dotty about dogs that she
overlooked her own daughter's claim to some part of the
estate. The new will gave Linus the sort of power that
would make it very difficult to plead dottiness, and if he
wasn't stopped, there might very well be yet another change
which would further strengthen his position and weaken
theirs. A sizable cheque now might well have been accepted
on the principle of a bird in the hand. Admittedly, George
Upperby had underestimated how much might be needed:
the interior of Linus's little artisan's cottage indicated
greater means than the outside suggested. Still, George was
no pauper and the possible gains were huge but somehow
that whole strategy had been side-stepped. It was very
galling.

Linus resisted with some difficulty the temptation to slam
the front door shut. He didn't want to give Upperby the
satisfaction of knowing he'd needled him. Back in the sitting-room he poured himself a very large whisky and made
no attempt to dilute it but he removed the coffee-cups in
the kitchen so that a reminder of Upperby's presence wasn't
staring him in the face as he drank.

His fury at the inferences Upperby had drawn was fuelled
by his own knowledge that he had done as much as possible
to disconnect himself from Mrs Egremont. He had had no
idea that she had changed her will and resented the suggestion that he had done so to further his own ends. When he
cast his mind back, he recalled that he had offered her some
advice but it had been disinterestedly offered and he had
been, as he had told her son-in-law, quite adamant that he
didn't want a part of it. But, as Upperby had remarked,
obviously not adamant enough. Since Mrs Egremont had
told her daughter the terms of her original will, she had
presumably told her about the changes. Linus couldn't help
wishing she had had the courtesy to tell him, too. It hadn't

been easy refuting a charge when the accuser appeared to be in possession of all the facts and he had none of them.

He reached out to the telephone, intending to ring Mrs Egremont and asked her exactly what the revised will contained, at least in so far as it involved him, but then he withdrew his hand. There was such a thing as cutting off your nose to spite your face: he had gone to some lengths to distance himself from Mrs Egremont's tendrils; if he phoned her now, he would be unravelling his previous efforts. He had a shrewd idea that her response would be to insist he went over to talk about it and that was the very thing he didn't want to get into. No, better to let sleeping dogs lie and hope that she would later settle upon a more sympathetic recipient of whatever favours had so infuriated her son-in-law.

By the time Linus had nearly finished his drink, much of his anger against George Upperby had evaporated. The man's fury, whether it was entirely on behalf of his wife or not, was understandable and Linus couldn't help thinking that, had their positions been reversed, he might have felt the same, though he hoped he would have behaved differently. Linus himself felt that, while it would have been entirely laudable to settle a comfortable amount on each dog, sufficient to enable the interest to support the animal with the capital going to some charitable organization after its death, it really was a bit extreme, not to say downright dotty, to leave one's entire—and very considerable—fortune to be divided among disparate individuals solely because they had bred one's dogs and were prepared to take them in, something which, in Linus' opinion they should have done without the lure of money.

He cast his mind over the other people involved. With the exception of Kevin Dedham—who was not, strictly speaking, the breeder anyway—he couldn't imagine any of them refusing to take their dogs back without the lure of finance. Sharon Dedham would certainly have done so, if she had been able to resist her husband's pressure. He wasn't quite so sure about the Chilton-Foliats. They were the sort who were clever enough to make the right noises while not necessarily practising the precepts they preached.

None of these considerations got him much further towards his goal of being shot of Mrs Egremont and her financial arrangements. The only thing he could be certain of was that seeing her would be counter-productive. No one talked Mrs Egremont out of something unless she wanted them to, and contacting her would result in a loss of freedom. Better by far to do nothing and hope that time, and her sense of his lack of interest—something which he felt confident he could rely on the Upperbys to draw her attention to at every opportunity—would result in another change to her will. And if it didn't, then at least he would be able to fulfil its terms with the least possible inconvenience to himself.

CHAPTER 6

'My dear, fancy you getting all the way up here,' Julian Treorchy said to Sharon Dedham as she struggled into the Ingliston showground with her dog cages mounted on a trolley made out of an old pram frame. It was a sharp contrast with his own gleamingly purpose-built one.

'I know. Aren't I lucky?' she replied. 'I don't know what came over Kevin. Well, I do—he had a little windfall on the pools and told me I could enter and he even gave me the petrol money to put by so that it wouldn't all be spent before the show came up.'

'A case of spend, spend, spend, I assume,' Julian said. 'Does this mean a mink coat and a white Jaguar?'

Sharon looked dismayed. 'No, no, it wasn't that sort of

a sum. Just big enough to be a very pleasant surprise and to put Kev in a good mood for nearly a week.'

'No mean achievement,' Ted Blandford murmured from behind his friend who was, perhaps fortunately, the only one to hear it.

'And does this little windfall enable you to stay over at a motel or B and B?' Julian asked, knowing quite well that Scotland and back in a day, with a dog show in between was, if not impossible, certainly not something most people would tackle.

'No, we couldn't run to that, not with some of the other things Kev needed to do with the money. He borrowed a friend's van and we'll find a lay-by and sleep in that.'

'Well, that'll be an interesting experience,' Julian commented with an inner shudder.

Sharon chuckled. 'Interesting rather than comfortable, I suspect. Still, it's the nearest I'm going to get to a holiday and you know what they say about gift-horses.'

When Kevin eventually joined her, he hung indecisively around the benches, obviously neither at ease nor remotely interested in the people, their conversation or their dogs. He stuck it for about a quarter of an hour, during which his discontent metamorphosed into surliness and then announced that he was off 'to see a man about a dog', and disappeared.

Ted Blandford watched him go. 'I'd have thought there were plenty of men and dogs around here,' he said acidly.

'That's just the way of saying he's off to the pub,' Sharon said. 'In this case, it'll be the beer tent. I don't expect we'll see him again until it's time to go.' She didn't seem unduly perturbed at the prospect.

'Well, dear, you will have an exciting night in your little van,' Julian commented.

'Just as well he wasn't intending to drive back after the show,' Ted said.

Meriel Chilton-Foliat screwed up her face. 'What a

dreadful man,' she said in an undertone to Charles and another exhibitor.

Charles glanced over his shoulder. 'You know how I feel about poofters,' he said. 'Can't stand them. I sometimes think Hitler had the right idea.'

'Not Ted and Julian,' Meriel said scornfully. 'They're very nice men, if only you'd look beyond the obvious. No, I meant poor Sharon's husband.'

'Oh, him! Say no more. One wonders what the world's coming to when one sees his sort. She always seems genuine enough. Common, of course, but she deserves better than him.'

'One thing must give you very great satisfaction, Charles,' his wife said sweetly. 'No one would ever be able to overlook the fact that you're a snob.'

Their companion laughed, more with embarrassment than amusement and, sensing undercurrents with which he wasn't familiar, moved away to immerse himself in placing, with the precision of a brain surgeon, every strand of his dog's hair so as to present it in the ring to its utmost advantage.

'I do wish you'd be a bit more careful what you say,' Meriel hissed. 'You know how dog people gossip. Why can't you learn never to say something unless you want it to get back?'

'What makes you think I don't want it to? I don't give a damn what that Dedham fellow thinks and as for the other two, well, if they haven't cottoned on to my opinion yet, after all these years, then they're stupider than I thought—and I never thought either of them that.'

'I just wish you wouldn't keep on about it.'

Charles raised his hands as if in surrender. 'OK. Matter closed. I won't mention it again—not today, at any rate.'

Sometimes there are shows which prove to be one person's 'day'—a show where one person takes all the major awards, and it looked as if this was to be Sharon's.

Her dogs won every class for which they were entered and the sire of Mrs Egremont's latest acquisition won Best Dog. Sharon was over the moon and most of the exhibitors were sufficiently glad on her account for that pleasure to overlay their own natural disappointment. It was generally assumed that she would take Best of Breed and go forward to compete for the Group, simply because, in all breeds as a general rule but more particularly in coated ones, a good dog will usually beat a good bitch—and Sharon's dog was very good.

But nothing can ever be guaranteed at a dog show and Ted Blandford had a very good bitch. It showed with just that little bit more verve than Sharon's dog and took the Best of Breed award.

Sharon hid her disappointment well and congratulated the winning owner with a smile. It was Kevin, who had returned on an impulse from the beer tent somewhat the worse for wear, who took her defeat badly.

'Bloody queers,' he said. 'They all stick together. You've only got to look at the judge to know he's one of them. I've half a mind to Kennel Club him.'

'If you don't watch what you're saying,' someone said, 'it's you that'll be Kennel Clubbed. Haven't you ever heard of good sportsmanship?'

'Good sportsmanship, my arse. It's all balls. The name of the game is winning. Some of us try to do it with quality dogs. The ones that get there do it by the back door. The whole game's rigged.'

'Then stop playing it, if that's what you think,' a second bystander said.

Kevin swayed a little as he turned to look the speaker up and down. 'All very well for you. You're not short of a bob or two. Just you wait. We won't always be as poor as church mice. Time'll come when we can bribe judges with the rest of you.'

Among the general expressions of disgust a woman's sun-set-of-the-Raj voice could be clearly heard. 'If you got off your backside, out of the beer tent and did an honest day's work—if you know what one is—you might, at the end of the next twenty years, be in a position to do just that. As it is, I can't see you offering a bribe worth even looking at.'

This sally was greeted with laughter which went a long way towards lifting the tension of a very nasty incident, if only because it was so apt. Kevin Dedham was the only one who failed to see any humour in it at all.

'You may scoff,' he said. 'I'll have the last laugh, though. You'll see. We've got money coming to us, Sharon and me. We'll show you.'

Julian Treorchy pushed his way through the little crowd that had collected and took Kevin by the arm. 'Come on, Kevin, it's just the drink talking. Don't spoil Sharon's day. She's had a marvellous run and now she's sitting on the bench in tears because you're spoiling it for her. She's just as disappointed as you, you know—more so, probably, since they're her dogs and she's the one who's put in all the hard work. Come on. Let me get you some black coffee.'

Kevin Dedham snatched himself out of Julian's light hold. 'Keep your hands off me,' he snarled. 'I'm not one of your rent-boys.'

Julian refused to be goaded. 'You can say that again, duckie,' he said, deliberately and exaggeratedly camp. 'You're *much* too long in the tooth.'

Kevin fumbled in his pocket and fished out his car keys. 'I'm going back to the van,' he mumbled. 'Tell Sharon where I am.'

'Get in the back and sleep it off,' someone shouted as he stumbled off in the general direction of the car park.

'Show over, ladies and gentleman,' Julian said. 'Time to go home.'

Meriel was standing close behind him. 'You handled that very well,' she said. 'It was nasty for a while there.'

'Thank you. I learned long ago never to rise to the bait,

but sometimes it's difficult. If it hadn't been for Sharon, poor kid, I'd have let him hang himself and hoped the Kennel Club would suspend him.'

'Sharon doesn't deserve him, that's for sure,' Meriel agreed.

Linus had a broadsheet delivered but he didn't always get around to reading it and when he did, it was usually just the main items, the letters and perhaps the editorial. He always took it with him to work. As often as not it remained in the car, unread, for no other reason than that he worked straight through his lunch-time. On those occasions when he was able to have a lunch-break, he felt morally justified in making it an extended one, to compensate for all those days when there hadn't been one at all. That was when the paper got read from cover to cover. Well, almost. Linus had no interest whatever in the sports pages.

That was how it came about that he saw the item tucked away on one of the inside pages. Under the headline 'Homophobic Killing' it read:

Police in the Borders area of Scotland are investigating the death of dog breeder Julian Treorchy (39) in a road accident on the A74 near Beattock. Mr Treorchy was returning from the championship dog show at Ingliston, near Edinburgh, when his estate car went out of control and swerved across the central reservation, hitting an articulated lorry on the northbound carriageway. Mr Treorchy was killed instantly. The driver of the lorry, Michael Shefford (33) of Warrington died on his way to hospital and Mr Treorchy's companion, Edward Blandford (43) is said to be 'comfortable' in a local hospital. Six dogs belonging to Mr Treorchy and Mr Blandford were unharmed and are being looked after by a local dog breeder. They include one of the top winners at the Scottish Kennel Club show. Forensic tests are being carried out on the estate car to establish the cause of the accident. In view of the fact that anti-gay slogans had been sprayed on the car, foul play is not being ruled out. Mr Shefford's widow and two children have been taken to a relative's house.

Linus read it through again with the chill of disbelief that always attaches to learning of the sudden death of someone one knows. It was just possible that there could be two people with so distinctive a name as Julian Treorchy but not that they should both be dog breeders, let alone have a friend called Ted Blandford. He felt more upset than the depth of his acquaintance with either man warranted, and he guessed that this was due as much to the inference that the accident had been engineered as to the fact that it had happened.

He finished his coffee and drove to the nearest town, stopped at the first newsagent he came to and bought a selection of tabloids. It was the sort of story the tabloids loved. He wasn't disappointed. GAY CAR KILLS FATHER OF TWO was the most lurid of the headlines, though the others weren't far behind. Had Linus been a totally disinterested reader, he would have gained some intellectual entertainment in trying, as a vet, to work out what characteristics of composition or temperament made a car 'gay'—or, indeed, not 'gay'. It was a ludicrous adjective in that context. Or it would have been had it not been for the very nasty subliminal message that the lorry-driver's death had been a deliberate homosexual act. The ensuing article gave much the same facts as those in Linus's broadsheet but it was a much cleverer and less straightforward piece of journalism which left the reader's sympathies entirely on the side of poor Mr Shefford and with little to spare for the other victims. While appearing to throw their hands up in shock and horror that anyone could be killed because of their sexual preferences, the tabloids all managed to convey the message that, had they been 'straight', the accident would never have happened and Mr Shefford's children wouldn't be orphans. They went on about 'these dreadful fiends that have done this thing', in such a way that the casual reader might well assume the fiends were Julian and Ted rather than the unknown who had tampered with their car—if, indeed, it proved to have been tampered with at all.

It was all very disturbing and left Linus with what he could only call a nasty taste in his mouth. It also left him wanting to know the outcome and to that end he read his paper with greater assiduity over the ensuing days. He also bought one of the tabloids for further elucidation, though he despised himself for doing so.

It wasn't long before the papers reported that the brakes had been tampered with and that, since they'd been working perfectly well on the journey north, it was a reasonable assumption that they'd been tampered with either in the car park of the motel where Julian and Ted had spent the nights either side of the show, or in the car park of the dog show itself. The tabloid dismissed the latter possibility on the grounds of the number of other cars parked there and the thousands of people coming and going throughout the day, contrasting this with the emptiness of a motel car park at night.

On the face of it, this was a valid enough point but Linus recalled the dog shows he'd been to and particularly the state of the East of England one towards the end of the day. He had only the haziest of ideas how long it would take to tamper with brakes but if it didn't take long, the car park of a dog show was as good a place as any, especially towards the end of the day. Or around noon, he thought suddenly. By mid-day everyone had arrived, so there were unlikely to be newcomers around, the cars would be parked as close together as the attendants could persuade the drivers to get, and almost everyone would be in the ring, waiting to go in the ring or watching the rest of their breed judging. They wouldn't be going to and fro between the showground and the car park, and if someone wanted to tamper with a car, all the other cars would screen him with the very occasional exception. The papers were concentrating on the homophobic aspects of the case, aspects which the sprayed slogans underlined, and which left the field of possible suspects wide open.

However, if one took into account the feasibility of the tampering having taken place at the show, there was the further possibility that the perpetrator had been a disgruntled exhibitor. They weren't all good losers, though such cases of extreme bad sportsmanship which Linus had thitherto heard about involved action taken against dogs. There was, for instance, a very successful Chow which had been poisoned and he understood it was by no means unusual in breeds like Poodles and Afghans, where coat presentation was all-important, for successful dogs to have lumps cut out of their coats to ruin their chances. It would take a fair degree of hatred to kill, even indirectly, an owner.

It occurred to Linus that perhaps he ought to make this point to the police. It was an idea he quickly rejected: they weren't stupid and had almost certainly worked it out for themselves even if they hadn't mentioned it to the press, and in any case, Linus had a constitutional dislike of bringing himself to the attention of the police. In his experience they were deeply suspicious of anyone who tried to be helpful. His name had already come up, albeit briefly, in connection with the death of another Korean Palace Dog breeder, so perhaps the less he said, the better.

He decided it would do no harm to make sure he had an alibi: these days the police ran things through computers and that meant that his name would appear if they were looking for a connection through dogs. He checked his timesheets and heaved a sigh of relief: he had called in at Government Buildings on the morning of the show and again before he knocked off. The following day he had got to a farm at an unwontedly early hour at the farmer's request. He couldn't have got to Edinburgh and back within working hours or between finishing in the evening and checking those sheep.

Part way through the day he found himself wondering whether he ought to contact Mrs Egremont. She was bound to be upset and might again want his escort. No sooner had the thought occurred to him than he pushed it away. Keep out of it, he told himself. She's the last person you want to get in touch with. Remember how she clings.

He did. He also remembered that she was basically a very kind-hearted old lady and probably a very lonely one. She had been shattered by Janine Flatford's death. She was unlikely to be any less upset by Julian's. Besides—and here Linus couldn't resist a small frisson of malicious glee—it would so annoy George Upperby. He had never intended to further his acquaintance with Maud Egremont just to annoy her son-in-law but there was no denying it would be a most satisfying by-product. He picked up the telephone.

She was plainly delighted to hear his voice. 'How very kind of you to ring, Linus. I was debating whether to drop you a line but then I thought you were probably very busy and you've been so kind in the past that I didn't like to bother you. Now you've saved me the bother.'

'I read about Julian Treorchy's death in the paper and I guessed how upset you must be. I did wonder whether you'd like me to take you to the funeral, whenever it is.'

'That's very thoughtful of you but I'll pass, as they say these days. The thing is, I haven't been at all well lately and I couldn't face it.' She hesitated. 'There is one thing you could do for me, though.'

Linus's heart sank and he felt guilty at that reaction. 'If I can,' he said mendaciously.

'Ted Blandford's been moved to his local hospital and I'd very much like to visit him. It's a bit far to drive myself.

I'd have asked George and Winifred to take me but I don't want them to get the idea that I need them and, in any case, I don't think George would be very cooperative. He doesn't like gays, you see.'

'He's not unique in that respect,' Linus said.

'No, but he takes the view that if Julian and Ted hadn't been, no one would have had it in for them and Julian wouldn't be dead. In other words, they brought it on themselves.'

'A bit harsh,' Linus commented.

'So if you would be kind enough to take me, he needn't know anything about it and if he ever found out it would prove that I'm perfectly capable of managing my own affairs.'

'Whereabouts is this hospital?' Linus asked apprehensively. The A74 went down the west side of the country, Mrs Egremont lived on the east coast and he was nearer the west than the east.

'Not exactly on the doorstep,' she said warily.

'I was afraid of that. Tell me the worst: we may as well get it over with.'

'Shrewsbury.'

'Shrewsbury!' Linus made no attempt to disguise his dismay. He did a quick calculation. Three hours—two and a half if he was very lucky and the country's lorry-drivers were on strike—to Hunstanton, and three and a half or four was probably a more realistic time, at least four to Shrewsbury and four back, then the return journey to Oxford. It couldn't be done in one day. If he left one evening after work, spent the next day ferrying Mrs Egremont to Shrewsbury and back and then came home first thing the following morning, he could do it, though he'd rather do without the expense of two nights in an hotel.

'I've got some time owing me,' he said. 'I can get a day off.'

'You'll need more than that,' Mrs Egremont said. 'You'd

better come over the evening before and I'll put you up for a couple of nights.'

It was a thought—and a temptation. Mrs Egremont's house would be a great deal more comfortable than any hotel and without the bills. Even so, the price was too high. Linus valued his freedom and his independence. 'No,' he said. 'I'm not going to impose on you when you haven't been well. But I'll tell you what: you can pick up the tab for the meals we have out. Agreed?'

'With pleasure—and all your petrol. Don't forget that. If you change your mind about staying here, the offer still stands. Can you manage the day after tomorrow?'

'Probably, though it's a bit short notice. If you don't hear from me, I'll pick you up about nine.' He calculated that that would enable them to get to Shrewsbury in time to have lunch somewhere before visiting Ted, and allow for a cup of coffee and a sticky bun en route.

The thing that struck Linus was that Mrs Egremont seemed to have aged considerably since they last met. She looked tired and quite lacked the vitality that had characterized her before.

'You look as if you could do with a holiday,' he commented.

'I'm a bit run down, that's all. I really ought to get myself some iron tablets. I dare say I'm just a bit anæmic. I'm getting on, you know.'

'All the more reason to take care of yourself,' Linus replied. 'Maybe you should get someone to live in so that they could keep an eye on you.'

'And have them helping themselves to the silver when I wasn't looking? No, thank you. I'll manage without.'

'Get an agency to find someone. They'll check their credentials and see that their references are above-board.'

She shook her head. 'The temptations would be too great,' she said.

'You're paranoid,' Linus told her.

'Very likely,' she retorted with a return to something like her old spirit. 'I'm also alive and I've every intention of staying that way. Living alone guarantees it.'

'Very paranoid.'

'I once saw someone wearing one of those T-shirts with a message on. It said: *Just because you're paranoid doesn't mean they're not out to get you.* I thought how very true that was.'

Linus dropped the subject. He knew a dead horse when he saw one, and steered the conversation into more general channels instead.

They stopped for lunch at a restaurant which had a very interesting menu. Mrs Egremont ordered smoked salmon and said that it 'would do', but urged Linus not to let her small appetite interfere with ordering whatever he wanted for himself.

'It's one of the things about getting old,' she said. 'You don't need to eat as much.'

This was true but it struck Linus as a little odd, coming as it did from a woman who only a few months ago had enjoyed her food as much as anyone.

Ted Blandford was propped up in bed, his face puffy and swollen with the bruises turned to the lurid Technicolor shades contusions acquire before they finally fade away. One arm was in plaster and the corresponding leg was under a little cloche, so Linus deduced that was broken, too.

Mrs Egremont sat herself firmly down on the chair beside the bed and instructed Linus to find one for himself. Her bedside manner was, Linus decided, entirely original.

'Ted,' she said, 'you look absolutely awful. You look worse than I feel, and that lifts my spirits no end.'

'It's customary to jolly the sick along by telling them how well they look,' Linus protested, though he noticed her remarks didn't seem to have upset their recipient.

'Nonsense. People who are ill, but not *that* ill, like to be told they look it. What's the fun in being ill if all anyone ever says to you is that you're looking fine? It makes you wonder if they think you're swinging the lead. Very depressing. Annoying, too, if it isn't the case.'

Ted managed what was obviously a painful smile. 'She's right, you know. Something I'll have to try to remember next time I go sick visiting. Did you go to Julian's funeral?'

'No,' Mrs Egremont told him. 'I didn't feel up to it and I knew it would upset me. Cowardly of me, I suppose. It doesn't mean I didn't care, but I'm sure Julian will have realized that.'

'I'm sure he will,' Ted agreed.

'Does anyone know exactly what happened?' Linus asked.

'I don't think they do. I don't think even the police know the whole story. They know the brakes weren't working because I told them that. That's what happened, you see. The car accelerated of its own volition down that steep incline. It responded to the brake at first—partially, at any rate—and then not at all. I gather the fluid had drained out.'

'An accidental leak?' Linus asked.

'Apparently not.'

'Any idea who was responsible?'

'They think it was me.'

'*You?* But that's ridiculous,' Mrs Egremont said.

'You'd think so, wouldn't you?' he replied. 'I mean, I might have tampered with the brakes, but would I be likely to get in the car and drive home in it? And that's always assuming I'd know how to tamper with the brakes in the first place. They don't believe that, either.'

Linus, who knew enough about the internal combustion engine to be able to check his oil, full stop, understood perfectly. 'What motive are you supposed to have had?' he asked. 'Either to kill Julian or to commit suicide?'

'It seems we fell out. Julian told me to sling my hook and this was my way of getting back at him. The suicide was because I couldn't face the prospect of life without him.'

'I thought you were both very good friends,' Mrs Egremont said.

'So did I. So did Julian—or that's what he would say if he were in any position to say anything.'

'I shouldn't think that's what they really think at all,' Linus said. 'More probably they're trying to needle you into letting slip some bit of information—something you noticed, perhaps—that you don't even realize you've got, much less its significance. Didn't I read something about the car's being sprayed with anti-gay slogans?'

'The sort of thing you hear about. Not very nice when you find them on your car. We'd have sprayed them off there and then if we'd had any spray paint. As it was, we didn't have much choice but to travel home with them. We weren't looking forward to having to stop for a meal.'

'No, I imagine not. No ideas on that score?'

Ted shook his head with some difficulty. 'No. We'd had a successful day and in any competitive area there will be people who don't like being beaten.'

'Drastic way to demonstrate it,' Linus said.

'I don't think many people would quarrel with that.'

'But Ted,' Mrs Egremont said, 'who in our breed would do a thing like that?'

'I can't think of anyone that would,' he agreed. 'It just doesn't fit.'

Linus said nothing. In his experience there was always someone who would stoop to almost anything, but it seemed kinder not to say anything quite so cynical, so instead he directed the conversation towards a discussion of hospital food. It wasn't a particularly interesting conversation but it was a great deal less depressing.

One of the things that had concerned Linus ever since he learned of Julian's death was the effect it would have on the arrangements Mrs Egremont had made for her dogs in the event of her own death: with two of the breeders dead, it meant that any dogs she had bought from them were now unprovided for. If Mrs Egremont had appeared to be in better health, Linus would have left the matter to be raised on a future occasion, but she was so clearly unwell that he decided to raise it now.

This was not an easy decision, since it might be argued that the less the old lady had to worry about, the better. On the other hand, Linus knew her well enough to guess that it wouldn't be long before it occurred to her anyway and it might be less of a trial if she had someone to bounce ideas off.

'With Mrs Flatford and Julian Treorchy both dead,' he began, 'you'll have to make some other provision for the dogs you bought from them. What will you do? Leave them, and some money for their support, to a canine charity? That's probably the best solution if only because charities don't, on the whole, die.'

'I'm ahead of you, Linus,' she told him. 'My solicitor must think I'm going ga-ga: my will stayed constant for years; then I amended it to make you responsible for seeing to it that the dogs were being looked after all right. I changed it again when Julian was killed. You're an executor.'

It was a responsibility Linus could do without but if she'd made alternative provision for the dogs, it shouldn't be too onerous.

'Fine,' he said. 'I dare say I can manage that. Which charity is taking care of them?'

'I'm not trusting any of them,' she retorted scornfully. 'Goodness me, no: they'd stick the dogs in rabbit-hutches for the rest of their lives and spend the money on political campaigns like this expensive and totally unenforceable registration scheme which anyone with half a brain would realize will only penalize the people like me, who keep their

dogs in a responsible manner anyway, and wouldn't touch
the people they want to get at, who won't bother to register
in the first place. I'll tell you this, Linus: that scheme was
dreamed up by a man.'

Linus laughed. It was good to see a flash of her old spirit.
'Now be fair, it's opposed by the Kennel Club and that's
a predominantly male organization, too.'

'Don't be difficult,' she said. 'In any case, it doesn't alter
the fact that animal welfare is one thing, politicking is
another. No, I've made much more satisfactory
arrangements.'

'Do I get any hint of what they might be?' Linus asked.
'Or do I wait till I take up my executive duties?'

'I suppose you might as well know but I'm not telling
anyone about it this time and if you've got any sense,
neither will you. It's quite simple, really. I'm making the
same provision but, if a breeder can't take the dog back for
any reason—like being dead—their dogs and that share of
the money will go to you. You still get to oversee the other
dogs, of course.'

Linus was genuinely appalled. 'But you can't do that!
You can't leave fifty per cent of your entire estate to a total
stranger!'

'I'm not. I'm leaving it to you.'

'Same thing.'

'Nonsense. You're a friend, not a stranger.'

'Try telling that to your daughter and her husband!'

'I shan't have to. They won't know anything about it until
I'm dead and gone. But I have taken your advice: I've left
Winifred a bit of extra capital—not a lot, but enough to show
willing, and I've made it perfectly clear that I haven't left
George anything because he doesn't need it.'

'He's going to love that,' Linus commented drily.

'I don't suppose he'll like it at all,' she replied shrewdly.
'The fact remains that I dare say it'll mean rather more to
you.'

Linus silently reviewed the relative financial positions of George Upperby and himself and felt bound to agree. It made no difference to the awkwardness of his position. 'Don't you see? I'll seem like a con-artist who's latched on to some helpless, gullible, malleable old lady and persuaded her to leave everything to me.'

She snorted. 'No one who knows me would ever call me helpless, gullible or malleable,' she said.

'They will once you're dead and they've seen what you've done.'

She shrugged. 'I'm sure your shoulders are broad enough to cope.'

'I'd rather you changed it back again,' Linus insisted. 'I'm not playing the maid who says no but has it just the same, you know. I don't mind helping out. I don't even mind accepting a small honorarium or even reasonable expenses, but I just don't want the hassle of inheriting a large part of your estate.'

'So what is it you really don't want—the money or the hassle?'

'I certainly don't want the hassle. As for the money— well, I don't need it at all and if I'm absolutely honest, I don't really want it, either.'

'I'm afraid that's too bad because I don't think I could face going back to John Westwell and changing my will yet again.'

'Then I hope to goodness none of the remaining breeders die,' he said. 'Do you realize you've just given me the perfect motive for doing away with them?'

'So I have. What fun! Shall we decide how best to go about it?'

Linus shuddered. 'Don't even think it.'

When they got back to Hunstanton and turned into the drive, Linus recognized the Upperbys' car. Its occupants had the air of people who had been waiting a long time.

George and Winifred climbed out with the stiffness of joints that had set firm through inaction.

'I might have known you'd be here,' George Upperby said in scathing tones as Linus got out of his own car to open the passenger door.

'I can't imagine why,' Linus said, helping Mrs Egremont out.

'I thought I'd made it clear to you that I expected you to stay away from my mother-in-law,' George Upperby said. 'I should have realized you'd be looking after your investment.'

'What's this?' Mrs Egremont broke in. 'You told Linus to stay away from me?' She turned to Linus. 'Is this true?'

'He came to see me,' Linus admitted. 'And that was the general drift of his conversation. He seemed to think I was after your money. Since I wasn't, his visit had very little effect.'

'How long ago was this?'

'Some time back. You'd just changed your will.'

'And now you've changed it again,' George Upperby said.

Winifred came forward then. 'I think this is something we'd better discuss inside, don't you?' she suggested.

Mrs Egremont frowned. 'I'm not at all sure I want that husband of yours inside my house.'

'I don't suppose you do,' Winifred said. 'On the other hand, I'm sure you'd dislike even more having a row on the front doorstep, which is what you seem to be working yourself up for.'

Mrs Egremont shook off Linus's helping hand and stomped angrily up the steps to the front door. 'In there,' she said, throwing open the door to the drawing-room. 'Winifred, you can go and make us all a cup of tea.'

Winifred went without a word but returned almost immediately with a grubby envelope held gingerly between her fingers. 'This was on the kitchen table for you, Mummy,' she said.

Mrs Egremont glanced at it dismissively. 'It'll be from the decorators, I expect,' she said, and dropped it on to the coffee-table.

'Decorators?' George glanced round the room as if expecting ladders and rolls of wallpaper to jump out at him. 'You didn't say anything to us about decorators.'

'Why should I? It's my house and I'm perfectly capable of choosing my own decorations, thank you very much,' his mother-in-law retorted.

'What are you having done?' Winifred asked.

'Upstairs. Most of it, anyway. I've moved into your father's old room until they've finished. It seems to be taking weeks.'

'I dare say they're spinning it out as long as they can,' George told her. 'Anything to run up the bills.'

'You're not going to change Daddy's old room as well, I hope,' Winifred said anxiously. 'I always loved that room.'

'I wasn't, because he was always so proud of it. He went to enormous lengths to furnish it just so and I know every-thing in it is genuinely antique but I never did much like it—I don't go much for all that dark, ornate continental furniture.' She turned to Linus. 'Do you know, he even bought antique wallpaper for it. Well, for that and for the little study as well, but I quite like that paper. Very pretty. I can't say the same for the other. But I ask you—second-hand wallpaper. Did you ever hear of such a thing? Any-way,' she went on, not waiting for a reply. 'I've changed my mind. It's a most depressing room, I think I'll re-do it in blue.'

'That would be sacrilege, Mummy,' Winifred protested.

'Don't be silly. After all, if nobody ever changed anything we'd all still be living in caves. I'm not a bit surprised your father got very depressed after he moved in there perma-

nently. I thought it was just because he didn't like having
to admit that he wasn't . . . that he was older than he liked
to think he was, but now I'm inclined to suspect it was that
gloomy room. What's happened to the tea, Winifred?'

Her daughter disappeared and as the door closed behind
her, Mrs Egremont turned on her son-in-law. 'What's all
this about my having changed. my will again?' she
demanded.

'Well, haven't you?'

'Is it any of your business?'

'Perhaps not but it's Winifred's and I'm Winifred's
husband.'

'In my book that makes you responsible for her future
welfare, not me,' her mother snapped.

'If you feel like that, why have you increased the provision for her? Or was it to ease your conscience over what
you've left this man?'

'No, it was not,' Mrs Egremont declared indignantly. 'As
a matter of fact, it was Linus who said I hadn't been fair
to Winifred and upon reflection, I decided he was right.'

'So you have been pursuing your interest,' George said,
sneering in Linus's direction.

'I haven't, but you're in no mood to believe it,' Linus
said.

'I have to hand it to you: as con artists go, you must be
one of the best,' George told him.

'Why is it, George, that you always put the worst possible
construction on everything?' Mrs Egremont demanded.
'No, don't bother to answer that: I know exactly what you'll
say and it does you no credit. I've a much more important
bone to pick. How did you know I've changed my will
again?'

'It was an inspired guess—a guess which you've just
confirmed as accurate,' he said with a satisfied smirk.

'No, it wasn't. You knew some of the details. Now I

hadn't told a living soul about it until I told Linus this afternoon. So how did you know about it?'

Winifred's reappearance with the tea-tray diverted attention from the issue long enough to give George time to think. Linus, who was coming to the conclusion that it was very easy to underestimate George Upperby, was rather surprised that he couldn't come up with a more original explanation.

'I heard it somewhere,' he said. 'You must have mentioned it to someone else. After all, all your awful doggy friends knew about the earlier provisions.'

'Only this time I didn't.'

Winifred looked uneasy. 'Now, Mummy, you know your memory isn't what it was.'

'Oh, I know I don't always know what date it is, and I've been known to go to the hairdresser's on the wrong day, but I'm not ga-ga, and I certainly know that Linus is the only person I told and he hasn't had time to tell anyone else because he's been with me ever since I told him. No one else knew—except John Westwell, of course.' She paused. Her puzzled frown disappeared. 'John Westwell. Of course! I should have known. Well, I can soon dispense with his firm's services. There are plenty of solicitors about. I wonder if the Law Society can provide me with a list of those that *aren't* Masons? Probably not. Still, a good Jewish firm will probably be safe. I don't think your little lot accept Jews, do they?'

George Upperby was red with anger by this time, and Linus couldn't blame him. He decided it was time to intervene.

'Don't you think you're jumping to conclusions, Mrs Egremont?' he suggested gently.

'Of course I am, but that doesn't mean they're wrong.'

'But solicitors are under a sort of Hippocratic oath— total confidentiality and all that,' Linus pointed out.

'Quite right,' George said. 'It's more than John's licence to practice is worth to pass information on.'

'Only if it could be proved,' his mother-in-law said sharply. 'And since both you and he would strenuously deny it, and I dare say the people who looked into it would be of the same persuasion, it would be impossible to prove, wouldn't it?'

'It's no good, George,' Winifred said. 'Once she gets a bee in her bonnet there's no dislodging it. You might as well bang your head on a brick wall.'

'I'd get more satisfaction banging *her* head on a brick wall,' George said savagely.

'Yes, well, it's done now and ranting at her won't change her mind. We might as well go home. I don't want to end up barred from my own home.'

But George wasn't letting go quite that easily. 'You know what it is?' he went on. 'It's those bloody dogs. She got herself in with a right bunch of weirdos there. They're the ones who've twisted her values like this—and this is the man who's stepped in out of the blue and taken advantage of it,' he finished.

'Now you're being as unreasonable as she is, George,' his wife protested. 'They're not all weirdos. Some are quite normal. I mean . . . well, look at the Chilton-Foliats.'

The slight pause, as if reluctant to name them, and Winifred's heightened colour were probably due to her own reluctance to risk antagonizing her husband still further by mentioning another of the breeders of Mrs Egremont's stock, Linus decided, and he wasn't surprised at her husband's subsequent glowering expression.

'Them!' he snorted. 'They've got ideas bigger than their bank-balances.'

'Hardly a crime,' Linus put in.

'You'd be the one to know all about that, wouldn't you?' George snapped back and Linus wished he'd kept his mouth shut, given the circumstances.

'And it doesn't stop them being perfectly nice people,' Winifred added.

'Especially Charles, I suppose,' George said. 'Even if he's a Mason, too. Did you know that, Mother? Maybe you're going to accuse Westwell of telling him, too.'

Mrs Egremont had begun pouring the tea. Now she put the pot back on the tray and sighed. She looked suddenly very old, very frail and very tired.

'I've had enough of this,' she said. 'Go home, George, and don't bother to come back again. I don't want to see you again. Ever. Winifred, you're welcome whenever you want to come. This is your home and I hope loyalty to that —that parvenu won't stop you coming. But don't bring him with you. You can go and get your tea somewhere else. I dare say there's a Little Chef on the way back to Thetford.' She sat back with her hands folded neatly in her lap and stared over their heads at a point on the wall opposite, her mouth a straight, determined line. It was the most un-ignorable hint Linus had ever seen.

The four of them sat in unbroken silence for several minutes. Linus felt awkward, George and Winifred seemed understandably ill at ease. Only Mrs Egremont seemed unperturbed. Eventually they rose to their feet.

'I think we'd better be going,' Winifred said awkwardly. She hesitated as if unsure whether or not to kiss her mother goodbye, finally deciding against it. 'I'll give you a call in a day or two, Mummy,' she said. 'Maybe you'll be feeling a bit better by then.'

Nothing was said until the sound of the Upperbys' car had travelled down the drive, paused at the gate and then disappeared among the passing traffic. Linus stood up and picked up the tray. 'I'll make some fresh tea,' he said.

'I went too far,' Mrs Egremont said.

'You laid it on a bit thick,' Linus agreed. 'Don't worry. They'll come round.'

'I wouldn't want to lose Winifred.'

'I don't think you will.'

'You're a good boy, Linus.'

'"Young man" is a compliment. "Boy" is a bit too much to take—and "good boy" makes me sound like a dog,' he said.

She smiled wistfully. 'When you get to my age, it doesn't matter what you call people.'

'I wouldn't carry that philosophy too far, if I were you,' Linus warned. 'I won't be a tick. Are there any biscuits?'

'There's a tin in the larder. Chocolate digestives. I remembered that you like them.'

Linus laughed. 'Good. I'll regard them as chockie drops —a reward for being a good boy.'

There was no doubt that the altercation with George Upperby had taken its toll, Linus thought when he came back with the freshly made tea. 'You know,' he said as he put the tray down on the little table, 'they do have a point. You can't really blame George and Winifred for being upset. I'm a complete stranger. I'm almost as much a stranger to you as to them. You don't really know the first thing about me, yet you change your will so as to give me a disproportionate share.'

'I know more about you than you realize,' the old woman told him wearily. 'In the first place there's the fact that I'm a rattling good judge of character. Always have been. All right, all right—that's not "knowing" and I'm the first to admit I'm not likely to be infallible. I had you checked out.'

'You *what?*'

'I had you checked out. I hired a detective. Everything you told me about yourself was true. Now are you satisfied?'

Linus didn't know whether to be offended that she hadn't taken him totally on trust or to applaud her common sense. On balance, he decided the latter course was wiser.

'Perhaps if you'd told George that, he'd be a bit happier about it.'

'I doubt it. He'd still think it was unfair. Damn!' she exclaimed, examining the nails of her left hand. 'Over there, Linus. You'll find some scissors in the small drawer of the bureau. Would you fetch them for me?'

He did so and she trimmed off a broken nail, then extended the hand and examined it. 'Old age, I suppose,' she said. 'My fingernails have always been one of my little vanities. Now they keep splitting and breaking. I look as if I chew them.' She screwed her face up into an expression of repugnance. 'I make sure I have an egg every day and lots of jelly but it doesn't seem to make much difference.'

'Surely what shows is already dead—don't you have to wait for results until the old nails have grown out and the new tissue starts to come through? That takes several weeks.'

She cheered up immediately. 'Of course. I should have known that. Good—I'll persevere. Linus,' she went on, changing the subject abruptly, 'how else could George have known what was in my new will?'

Linus shook his head. 'I don't know. Are you really sure you didn't discuss it with anyone else?'

'Quite sure.'

'You don't have a friend—particularly a friend from the Thetford area—that you might have said something to about it?'

'The Chilton-Foliats are the only other people in that area that I know and I haven't seen them to tell even if I wanted them to know, which I don't.'

'You're sure? I mean, since they both obviously know each other and have you as a common denominator, what could be more natural than that it should come up?'

'Yes, isn't that odd? All these years and neither has ever mentioned that they knew the other. I wonder why?'

'Now for heaven's sake don't start getting paranoid about that!' Linus said hastily. 'Most probably each assumed the other would have mentioned it or took it so much for granted that it didn't need mentioning.'

'Mm. Odd, though. Not that it gets us any further forward. I didn't mention it to either party. I didn't even tell you till this afternoon, so it must have come from John Westwell.'

'It begins to look like it,' Linus admitted reluctantly.

'His father would turn in his grave if he knew. A very upright gentleman, John Westwell Senior. I suppose his son thought it was in his long-term interests to do George a favour.'

'It's irrelevant,' Linus pointed out. 'George was quite right. It's your word against theirs and I'm afraid they'll both be believed before you will. If you're quite certain you didn't mention it to anyone else, your only remedy is to change your solicitor.'

'So you don't believe me, either?'

'I don't think you're lying, if that's what you mean. I'm sure you believe you haven't mentioned it, but I can't exclude the possibility that you said something—probably something quite innocuous—to someone who either put two and two together and told George, or who repeated it to him and he did the adding-up sums. But if changing your lawyer makes you feel happier, then change him— and no,' he went on, anxious to forestall what he saw coming, 'I'm not going to recommend someone. That really would put the cat among the pigeons.'

'You mean another cat.'

Linus laughed. 'Yes, I suppose I do.' He stood up. 'Now I'm off back to my hotel. I've had a hard day's driving and I've got to be up early to get to work in the morning—and that's a three-hour drive, remember. Is there anything I can get you before I go?'

'I really am very tired,' Mrs Egremont said. 'Would you help me upstairs? I think I'll go to bed nice and early and read a good book. Bring the biscuit tin up in case I get peckish.'

'Shall I fill a flask with boiling water and bring that up? You could make coffee.'

'I've got a kettle up there for that. All mod. cons.'

Linus helped her to her feet and guided her as unobtrusively as he could up the stairs. He soon realized why she found William's room depressing. Unlike the rest of the house, there was no Georgian furniture here with its light lines. This room was heavily, darkly Victorian, ornate and solid. Despite the ornateness, it was an essentially masculine room, the dark mahogany of the wood accentuated by the dark green velvet curtains and upholstery. The wallpaper was also predominantly a strong green. Linus recalled that it had been bought as an antique and put up here. He was prepared to believe it, not because he knew anything at all about antique wall-coverings but because it was clearly apparent that it had been rolled or even folded at some time in its career: bits of green had flaked away giving a generally neglected air to the whole room. He could see that it might have struck a child as cosy, but he remembered the opening chapter of *Jane Eyre* and decided it might also have had that effect. Perhaps it was as well that Winifred had come into the first category.

'Blue would be a great improvement,' he said.

'Yes, wouldn't it?' Mrs Egremont agreed. 'This is such a *horrid* room. I'll get the decorator to let me have some samples in the morning. I could even send the furniture over to Winifred if she's so fond of it. What do you think?'

'And excellent idea,' Linus agreed with unkind glee. Winifred might have—or think she had—a sentimental attachment to it, but he very much doubted whether George would want to give it house room. It was a toss-up between whether they declined it on the grounds that they didn't have enough room for it or accepted it and packed it off post-haste to the auction rooms. Probably the latter, he decided. 'Now will you promise me one thing before I go?'

'Only so long as it's not to change my will all over again.'

'It's nothing to do with that. I want you to promise me you'll get the doctor to call. I don't want you being all independent and going to the surgery. Get him to come here. Insist on it. Tell him you feel under the weather and depressed and ask for a tonic.'

She seemed doubtful. 'I don't like doing that,' she protested. 'You see, he's an old man. He retired from general practice years ago but he still sees one or two elderly patients—people like me who just don't fancy putting our lives in the hands of bright young things who think they know better than we do what's good for us.'

'Couldn't be better,' Linus told her. 'He'll listen to you with the sympathy of a contemporary.'

'Yes, but I don't like calling him out when it's not an emergency.'

'Look,' Linus said patiently, 'it's obvious to me that you're not as fit or as happy as you used to be. Now maybe that's just advancing years. If so, then that's what he'll tell you. But it may be something else, something that's quite simple to put right—and he's the one who will be able to do something about it. Give him the chance. In any case, I dare say he'll enjoy the chat. Promise?'

'I'll think about it. If I get any worse, I will.'

'And if you need any help, don't be too proud to ask Winifred to come over.'

'Not you?'

'Not me. For one thing it would take me three hours to get here, which is less than helpful. For another, Winifred's your daughter and she'd like to be asked. Besides, it's her duty.'

'And not yours.'

'Precisely.'

'Despite my will?'

'Don't start trying to blackmail me with that. What you

do with what you've got is entirely up to you. If you want
to go out tomorrow and change it, that's fine by me, but
I've a life of my own to live and I'm not living it dancing
to your tune on the off-chance you leave me something.
Clear?'

'Very.'

'Good, then I'll be off. You get that doctor in.'

CHAPTER 7

Linus was confident that if Mrs Egremont took his advice
and saw her doctor, it wouldn't be long before she was in
better spirits and consequently more inclined to re-consider
the arrangements she had made for the disposal and continued welfare of her dogs. He hoped that his words would
bear fruit and she would decide to make a less contentious
will under the terms of which the major beneficiary became
a charity. Not all of them had political aspirations and he
toyed with the idea of sending her details about them. He
rejected it: the last thing he wanted to be accused of was
continuing to exert pressure, though he suspected he would
stand condemned no matter what he did. More importantly, perhaps, he didn't want Mrs Egremont thinking that
her most recent allocation of her estate had made him feel
obliged to dance increased attendance on her—and he
wasn't at all sure that that result was just what she had
had in mind when she had told him about it. Mrs Egremont
was not above a bit of emotional blackmail if it would serve
her purpose.

He was less sure what to make of any relationship
between the Upperbys and this John Westwell. Brought up
from childhood with a deep-seated belief in the absolute
professional discretion of doctors, lawyers and priests, he
found it difficult even to consider the possibility that other

considerations might take precedence. Yet if Mrs Egremont was telling the truth, what other explanation could there be? Linus was quite sure she wasn't lying when she said she had told no one else, but he couldn't exclude the possibility that she might have said something from which, perhaps as much in her choice of words as in the sentiment expressed, the facts had been deduced. Perhaps she had said something, innocuous in itself and of no significance to its intended audience, which had been picked up by a bystander to whom it conveyed rather more. This was by no means improbable, since Mrs Egremont had, like many elderly and slightly deaf people, a tendency to raise her voice higher than was strictly necessary.

Nevertheless, she was adamant and since she was in full possession of all her faculties—apart from that slight auditory impairment—he saw no real reason to doubt her word. Which brought him back to her solicitor. The most charitable interpretation of events must cast some doubt on his professional integrity. Linus hoped Mrs Egremont would pursue her stated intention of transferring her legal business elsewhere. This, too, was not something he was inclined to urge her to and for precisely the same reasons.

He could only hope that time would solve the problem: that Mrs Egremont would get herself a new solicitor and make a new will under the terms of which Linus would either not figure at all, or would be given a purely consultative role. As things were, he stood to inherit at least half of the residue of her estate and while he could doubtless find a use for the money, not least to enable him to buy pictures, he found it an embarrassing position to be in and would be very happy to have the embarrassment removed.

Linus had a television but he very rarely watched it. Even more rarely did he turn it on for background companionship. It was therefore entirely by chance that he heard of Sharon Dedham's death.

He had turned the television on for the nine o'clock news but he was only listening to it with half an eye because his attention had been caught by a fascinating article in the *Veterinary Record* about a possible familial element in diseases of the canine auto-immune system. His mind registered the unsurprising fact that the government was confident in the progress of the economy and the equally predictable opinion of the opposition that the government had got it wrong. It hardly ranked as news, Linus thought, much less warranted headline status. The details were of no interest to him and his veterinary article soon blurred even that degree of awareness.

It was the name that brought his attention back to the screen with a jolt, only to find that he had missed the initial explanatory statement. He knew the name and if the house that appeared on the screen wasn't the one he had visited with Mrs Egremont, then it was one very similar. Not that that meant a great deal: there must be tens of thousands of such houses on exactly similar estates up and down the country. Still, the fact that the husband was called Kevin seemed to clinch it and, since he had been charged with her murder, it looked like a sad little tale of domestic violence which would soon be forgotten by everyone not immediately involved. Linus did not consider himself uninvolved. If it was the same Sharon, then he now stood to inherit even more of Mrs Egremont's estate.

'Oh God,' he murmured. 'Let it be another Sharon Dedham.'

He switched channels to catch the ten o'clock news and this confirmed his fears. Sharon had apparently been beaten to death and the police had taken away a monkey wrench and a pickaxe handle as well as her husband.

'Poor silly cow,' Linus said, switching off the set.

He wasn't surprised to get a phone call later that night from Mrs Egremont who was understandably very upset.

'Linus, have you seen the news this evening? About Sharon's murder?'

'Yes, I saw it. It is the same Sharon, I take it?'

'Of course it is. Oh, Linus, I feel so responsible! Do you think I should go to the police?'

'Whatever for? I thought they'd arrested that awful Kevin?'

'Yes, they have—dreadful man.'The thing is, I can't help feeling it's all my fault.'

'Now you're just being silly,' Linus said firmly. 'Heavens above, he's a nasty enough character with a track record for violence, according to gossip. There doesn't seem to be much doubt about it. Where do you come into the picture?'

'I've been putting two and two together. I thought what I was doing was for the best. Now I'm not so sure. Linus, I bought my dogs from four different breeders and I let it be known that money would be settled on them when I was dead so that they could take the dogs back and not be out of pocket over it. There wasn't any secret about it, nor about the fact that if anyone wasn't able to take back the dogs they bred, the money would be divided up between those who did. Three of those four breeders are dead. Maybe that's why they were killed.'

'But all three deaths were quite different. Don't detectives always look for a similarity of method?'

'So they always say in the papers but I've never understood why. If I wanted to murder a succession of people, the one thing I'd make jolly sure I didn't do would be to use the same method.'

The same thought had often occurred to Linus. 'Perhaps most murderers aren't very bright,' he suggested. 'Or perhaps, having found a method that works, they stick to it.'

'Quite possibly. The thing is, both Janine and Sharon were beaten to death.'

'Mrs Flatford was mugged,' Linus said.

Mrs Egremont had no difficulty disposing of that

inconvenience. 'A red herring,' she said. 'That's what everyone was supposed to think—that it was a random attack by a mugger. But it's just the sort of thing Kevin Dedham would be capable of.'

'So you accept that he killed his wife?'

'Shouldn't think there's any doubt of that. And another thing: Julian's brakes were tampered with and that show was one of the few that Kevin took his wife to.'

'But Julian wasn't bludgeoned to death,' Linus pointed out.

'No. Exactly. And who better to tamper with someone's brakes than a motor mechanic?'

And where better to do it than the car park of a dog show, Linus thought. Then he shook his head. 'It still doesn't make sense,' he said. 'After all, if his intention was to get rid of the opposition, it would be Meriel Chilton-Foliat he'd have done in, not his wife. Surely Sharon is the registered breeder?'

'Yes.'

'Then killing her would be counter-productive—the money would go to Mrs Chilton-Foliat, and I can't see her killing anyone, can you?'

'Well, no, not really. I suppose it's conceivable that she might stick a hatpin between someone's ribs or lace their tea with arsenic, but I can't imagine her doing anything really violent or underhand.'

Linus, who thought that a hatpin between the ribs was fairly violent and arsenic in the tea was decidedly under-hand, refrained from contradicting her, partly because he knew what she meant. 'I know it seems improbable,' he said, 'but I think we have to accept that these three deaths are all unconnected. It's just a sad coincidence that you happen to have bought dogs from each of them. Look at it another way: think of all those people who've been mur-dered or have met with nasty accidents that weren't entirely accidental, and ask yourself how many of them you'd bought dogs from. You can only make the connection because you happen to know the people.' This was a flawed argument and Linus knew it. He hoped Mrs Egremont would be too happy to jump at the consolation it offered to analyse it too closely.

'So you don't think I need warn Meriel to be on her guard against Kevin?'

'No, I don't. For one thing, he's in police custody and given his track record, I shouldn't think they'd let him out on bail. Even if they do, what would be the point in his attacking her? With Sharon dead, he's blown any chance of her share of the money.'

'You don't think I should tell the police of the connection between the three of them?'

'You can if you want to. If it will make you feel easier, perhaps you should. I can't honestly say that I think it will do any more than confuse the issue. How are you in yourself? Apart from worrying about this, I mean.'

'I'm a lot better. I took your advice and got old Dr Knottingley in. He said the same as you: that William's room was depressing and I should move back into my own room as quickly as possible. So I did. It was only a matter of getting the decorators to move the furniture back in. They weren't very pleased about it—kept muttering about not being removal men—but the extra pay seemed to go a long way towards soothing their pride. He's put me on a tonic and is having blood tests done. He's sent some hair off, too. I thought hair-loss was just another sign of advancing age but he said it sometimes meant a vitamin deficiency, so he's testing for that as well. Still, that's all academic, really. I feel so much better that I'm convinced it was just that dreary room. Who'd have thought it?'

'I can't pretend to know much about psychology,' Linus said, 'but I remember years ago reading an article about the influence of colour. Apparently, if you decorate a restaurant in shades of apricot, people order more because that range of shades encourages them to feel hungry. Mind you, I can't say I've noticed that many restaurateurs seem to have read the same article.'

'Dr Knottingley said much the same: he said it wasn't a coincidence that so many bedrooms were pink. He said it made people feel warm and cosy.'

Linus who, like most men, was not smitten by pink bedrooms, declined to be drawn into that one and, having ascertained that there was nothing else she wanted from him, told her to take care of herself and then hung up.

The conversation gave him much to think about. He hadn't hitherto given any thought at all to the possibility of a link between the three deaths and he was, in any case, quite sure that Sharon's death was unconnected with the others if only because he could not believe that a Kevin who was cunning enough to kill Janine and Julian through diverse means to the same end would be stupid enough, even in a fit of temper, to kill his only passport to Mrs Egremont's money. The fact that the old lady had changed her will was irrelevant because Kevin presumably knew nothing about it. Even Linus wasn't entirely sure of its provisions. In particular, he didn't know what, if any, provision Mrs Egremont had made should he predecease her.

It didn't really make much difference unless Mrs Egremont had taken his advice and changed it yet again in favour of a charity. Until and unless she did that various people were at risk, the degree of risk depending entirely on how familiar others were with the current arrangements.

He was the best candidate. If he disposed of Meriel Chilton-Foliat, Winifred Upperby and then Mrs Egremont, he stood to become a very rich man indeed. If he were a detective looking for a motive, he would be his own prime suspect.

Meriel, who had just as good a reason to dispose of Janine Flatford and Julian Treorchy, and to heave a sigh of relief at Sharon Dedham's disappearance from the contest, would now only have to get rid of Mrs Egremont. That was if

Meriel thought the original bequests still held. If not, she would dispose of Linus, too. Like Mrs Egremont, Linus couldn't quite see her doing it. He was less sure about Charles who might have had an incentive on his wife's behalf.

On the other hand, the Upperbys had every reason to want to get rid of the lot of them. Linus could no more see Winifred killing any one—least of all her own mother—than Meriel. Winifred was too . . . he searched for the word . . . too *bourgeois*. George was another matter altogether. George would certainly see it as in his wife's—and therefore indirectly his own—interests to get rid of Linus, and if he were afraid Linus's death would lead Mrs Egremont to make yet another will to Winifred's disadvantage, Linus didn't think he would have too much compunction about doing away with his own mother, much less his mother-in-law.

Only if Mrs Egremont could be persuaded to leave everything to a canine charity or to Winifred with instructions that dogs must be taken care of, with someone appointed to see that they were, only then would everyone's motive for murder be buried. George might not be happy at seeing the bulk of the Egremont estate going to charity but at least a charity was something one couldn't murder, though one could challenge it in the courts—a very expensive and uncertain undertaking.

Linus would have to broach the subject again and take the risk that she would simply stick obstinately to her present position. He would have to push the advantages of a permanent solution to the dogs' welfare: the fact that charities don't die and the bigger ones are unlikely to go bust; the fact that Winifred would be unlikely to ignore her mother's wishes, especially if she were overseen by someone like Mrs Egremont's own vet—a choice that would raise fewer hackles.

What he dared not even hint at was any suspicion that

he gave credence to her theories of murder, much less that she might herself be at risk. He supposed it could be argued that if there were a risk, then she should be on her guard. But against what? Was anything to be gained by making her afraid to go out in case she was mugged? Afraid to drive anywhere in case someone tampered with the Armstrong-Siddeley's brakes? Or afraid to go to bed in case she was clubbed to death by a presumed burglar? No, if someone were determined to kill her—and that was by no means certain—forewarned would be simply worried. It wouldn't be forearmed.

Nor could Linus take his theoretical possibilities to the police. Either they'd already come to the same conclusion, in which case they'd get to him sooner or later, or they hadn't and in that case his putting the idea into their heads would be interpreted as a very cunning ploy on his part to divert suspicion towards someone else.

God, Linus thought, holding his head in his hands. This is paranoia. Worse. It's paranoia gone mad. It's not very far removed from the thought process that sees little green men everywhere and tells the police. People murder on the spur of the moment. Either that or they follow a pattern. Everyone knows that. It's not just folklore. There have been three tragic deaths unconnected by anything except that an old woman in Hunstanton bought a dog or two from each of them.

And that they knew one another.

Stop it! he told himself sharply. Forget it. Put the whole silly business out of your mind. Now. You've plenty of work to do. Get on with it. Do what you swore you would do— keep well away from Mrs Egremont and pray that she sees sense and makes the alterations of her own volition. If you don't go out of your way to show any interest in her or her dogs, maybe she'll take huff and change her will in a fit of pique.

*

It took him a moment or two to place the two men who stood at his door. Rievaulx. That was it. Detective-Inspector Rievaulx. The rather aristocratic name was somewhat at odds with the decidedly Norfolk accent. The other man was his sergeant but Linus couldn't recall his name.

The Inspector put him out of his uncertainty. 'We have met. Detective-Inspector Rievaulx, and this is Detective-Sergeant Chacombe.'

'I remember. I take it you want to come in?'

'It would be sensible, don't you think?' the Inspector said, glancing at the houses on either side.

Linus stood aside and followed them into the sitting-room. 'Tea? Coffee?' he asked.

'That would be very kind. We didn't have time to stop for a cuppa at St Aldate's. We were held up on the A43.'

'Air Force moving all their heavy equipment?' Linus said conversationally.

Rievaulx laughed. 'The voice of experience,' he commented.

'I used to think they only did it when they saw me coming,' Linus replied from the kitchen. 'Then I discovered that everyone in the county had the same idea. It's a fast enough road if you've got it to yourself but too narrow to overtake on.'

He brought a tray of coffee-mugs and a sugar-bowl in and set it down. 'I don't imagine this is a social visit,' he said. 'Why are you here?'

'It's in connection with a Mrs Maud Egremont. You know her, I believe.'

'You know perfectly well I do: I took her to Mrs Flatford's funeral.'

'When did you last see Mrs Egremont?'

'I'm not sure. I'd have to look it up to be precise.'

'Would you hazard a guess?'

'Several weeks ago. At least four.' He paled. 'Oh my God, don't say something's happened to her.'

'Now why should you assume that, Mr Rintoul?' the Inspector said, his tone deceptively benign.

'She's in her eighties and when I last saw her, she hadn't been at all well. It was a natural fear, given the circumstances.'

'What did you think was wrong with her when you saw her?'

'I've no idea: I'm a vet, not a physician. I advised her to get her doctor in.'

'And did she?'

'How should I know? I live a hundred and thirty-one miles away.'

'You didn't telephone?'

'No.'

'That wasn't very friendly, was it? A phone call wouldn't have hurt you.'

'Mrs Egremont is a very old lady and I suspect she's quite a lonely one, Inspector. As a consequence, she's a bit inclined to . . . to cling. I know it sounds selfish and unkind not to want to get too involved and maybe I'm both those things, but I have been to some pains to distance myself from her.'

'So you've had no contact with her since then?'

'I haven't seen her but she did ring me—oh, a couple of weeks ago. Someone she knew, a Sharon Dedham, had been beaten to death by her husband and Mrs Egremont was very upset.'

'You didn't know this Sharon Dedham?'

'I'd met her. I wouldn't say I knew her. I went with Mrs Egremont to check over a puppy she was thinking of buying.'

'Do you know the terms of Mrs Egremont's will?'

'In general, yes. In detail, no. That's to say I know what

she told me they were but I haven't seen a copy and I've no idea whether she's changed it.'

'My understanding is that you'll come out of it rather well.'

'So I'm told. Would you believe me if I told you I've tried to persuade her to change it in favour of a canine charity?'

'Frankly, Mr Rintoul—no.'

Linus couldn't blame him. 'That's also part of the reason why I've kept away: I hoped she might feel neglected and change it out of pique. I also didn't want her family accusing me again of "nursing my investment".'

'Has that been said in the past?'

'Something to that effect. Those might not have been the precise words.'

'Do you blame the family for thinking that?'

'No. In their shoes, so would I. Look, Inspector, I realize you're not asking questions out of idle curiosity, but I would like to know what they're leading up to. What has happened to Mrs Egremont?'

'My latest information is that Mrs Egremont is alive, well, and thriving.'

'Good. Then why this visit?'

'You might say we're acting on information received.'

'From whom? Concerning what?'

'Concerning Mrs Egremont. You obviously knew she was ill. Did she describe her symptoms?'

'She was depressed. She looked anæmic and she was tired.'

'Nothing else?'

'Nothing I can think of. I know various minor things were wrong but she's an old lady: things tend not to work quite so well as they age. People aren't any different from cars in that respect.'

'You know about cars, do you, Mr Rintoul?'

'As a matter of fact, I don't. I'm something of a mechanical moron. I do know that the older they are, the more likely they are to go wrong. I've learned that from first-hand experience.'

'Did she mention hair-loss?'

Linus thought. 'I believe she did, but hair tends to thin with age, anyway.'

'True.' The Inspector consulted his notebook. 'And brittle finger nails?'

Linus cast his mind back and frowned. It rang a bell. 'I took her to see someone in hospital and a nail broke. She said they'd been doing that and she was eating eggs and jelly. I gather she'd always prided herself on her nails.'

'And didn't all these things add up to a medical man like you?'

Linus shook his head. 'I can't see any connection.'

'Well, I suppose you'd be unlikely to say anything else,' the Inspector commented affably. 'Tell me: prior to deciding not to see Mrs Egremont in the hope that she'd alter her will in favour of someone else, how often did you see her?'

'Hardly at all. I took her to Shrewsbury to visit Ted Blandford in hospital and that was the first time I'd seen her since Mrs Flatford's funeral.'

'This hospital visit must have taken up several days of your time.'

'One whole day and an afternoon before and a morning after. That's all.'

'So you stayed there for two nights?'

'No. I value my independence. I stayed at a small hotel.'

'I don't suppose you happen to remember what it was called?'

'Of course I do.' Linus went into the kitchen and rooted around in a drawer until he found what he was looking for. He put the credit card receipt down on the coffee-table. 'There you are, Inspector. I haven't kept the bill because

it wasn't deductible but I'm sure the hotel will verify that
I had two dinners and two breakfasts there.'

'Thank you, Mr Rintoul,' the Inspector said, handing
the slip to his sergeant who duly recorded the details.

'Inspector, don't you think you could tell me what this
is all about? Just a hint of what's bothering you?'

The Inspector ignored the question. 'Do you have much
to do with arsenic in your professional work, Mr Rintoul?'

'None at all. What would I use it for?'

'Killing vermin, perhaps?'

'Inspector, I'm sure you're as well aware as I am that
that's the responsibility of the local authority. Farmers do
it themselves, of course, but they use Warfarin, dogs or
shotguns. Nobody uses arsenic these days.'

'But you could get hold of it if you needed it.'

'I suppose so. I've never tried. I don't even know if chem-
ists stock it. I doubt it and even if they did, I'd have to
sign for it so it would soon be checkable.' He frowned. 'Does
this mean you think Mrs Egremont has been poisoned?'

'Why should you assume that, Mr Rintoul? Or do you
have some reason for thinking we might have good grounds
for believing so?'

Linus exhaled with sharp exasperation. 'For God's sake,
Inspector, don't take me for a fool. I'm quite sure you've got
better things to do than waste your time and the tax-payer's
money coming all this way to ask pointless questions. If
you're asking me about Mrs Egremont and then, in the
next breath, about my access to arsenic, you can hardly be
surprised if I deduce that there might, just possibly, be
a connection between the two. So I'll cut some of the
meanders out of this little session: when I last saw Mrs
Egremont, we had several meals together, all of them in
public places, but I suppose I would have had the chance
to slip some arsenic into her food. For what it's worth, I
didn't and I don't have the foggiest idea how much arsenic
it would take to kill someone. Quite a bit, I imagine. Still,'

he went on as a thought struck him, 'that's not much of a defence, is it? I mean, if she's well and thriving, I obviously can't have given her enough.'

Inspector Rievaulx permitted himself a tight smile. 'In cutting across the meanders, as you put it, Mr Rintoul, you appear to have created an ox-bow lake in which you could well drown. Our method may be excruciatingly slow but going with the current usually gets you there in the end.'

Linus sighed. 'Point taken, Inspector. We'll do it your way.'

'Thank you, Mr Rintoul. You appear to be thinking of acute arsenical poisoning. Are you aware that there is a chronic form—the administration of small doses over a prolonged period?'

'I'm a vet, Inspector. I do know the difference between acute and chronic.'

'My apologies. I'm sure you do. The thing is, do you know the difference between the symptoms of each when it comes to arsenical poisoning?'

'I don't know the symptoms of either. In fact, I wasn't aware there was a chronic form. I thought the Borgias gave themselves small doses every day to increase their resistance to it so that any dose administered by a third party would have to be so massive that they'd detect the taste.'

'Fascinating, Mr Rintoul. I didn't know that. I thought they employed tasters?'

'I believe they did but I suppose if you live in the sort of society which makes you need to employ a taster, your paranoia wouldn't lead you necessarily to trust him implicitly.'

'You've obviously looked into the matter.'

'Not at all. It's something I read when I was a boy. One of those fascinating, but useless, sidelights on history.'

'Quite.' Inspector Rievaulx grew thoughtful. 'By administering it to themselves, they could control the dosage. Maybe that way you avoid actually being poisoned. The thing is, Mr Rintoul, what opportunity have you had to administer small doses to Mrs Egremont over a prolonged period of time?'

'None. As an academic exercise, I have had two or three opportunities to slip small amounts into food or drink, or to slip her a massive, lethal dose, but prolonged poisoning? No. Besides,' he went on as a thought struck him, 'there wouldn't have been any incentive to do either until I learned about her most recent change of will—and I certainly don't go about with arsenic in my pocket on the off-chance of meeting someone I need to murder, and I haven't seen her since. If somebody's poisoning Mrs Egremont, it isn't me. Is arsenical poisoning what her doctor says it is?'

'Apparently.'

'"Apparently",' Linus echoed. 'So you've had this from a third party. Let me speculate. I advised Mrs Egremont to see her doctor. She's taken my advice and he thinks she's suffering from chronic arsenical poisoning. At a guess, it isn't proven yet, or your choice of words would have been different, though you might simply be even more devious than the average professional detective. Let's assume you're being quite puritanically truthful. If the doctor didn't inform the police, either he doesn't suspect foul play, which is odd, or maybe he takes his Hippocratic oath very literally indeed, so who does know and who told you? He might have mentioned it to Mrs Egremont even at the risk of upsetting her, and I suppose he might have mentioned it to her daughter, though that brings us up against the Hippocratic oath again. Or Mrs Egremont might have told her. Either way, Winifred would have gone straight home and told her husband. Which brings us to who told you. It might have been Mrs Egremont. More probably her son-in-law.'

'Why?'

'Because if you start asking her questions, she'll realize there's a suspicion I poisoned her and be that much more likely to change her will again, this time in Winifred's favour—possibly even with a mention of George, though I don't think he's daft enough to rate that possibility very highly.'

'So you're not suggesting he might be poisoning her?'

Linus considered the matter. 'I can't say why he should. He might want to poison *me*, but he will want her dead eventually, anyway, though I'd have thought he'd have been willing to let time take its natural course. He certainly wouldn't want her dead *before* she changed her will.'

'So he knows what's in the will?'

'I think he knows in greater detail than I do.'

'Is it general knowledge?'

Linus shook his head. 'I don't think so. Mrs Egremont said she hadn't told anyone except me.'

'She must have told her daughter or her son-in-law.'

'She insists not. She reckons her solicitor told him.'

'Hardly professional conduct.'

'Quite. She attributes it to their both being Masons.'

There was a pause while the Inspector digested this. 'Would you describe Mrs Egremont as being a somewhat . . . eccentric . . . old lady?'

'Eccentric—yes; stupid—no.'

'So Mr Upperby has a good motive for implicating you, if not for poisoning his mother-in-law. Let's assume the story of the poisoning is true; let's even go further and assume you're not the one responsible. Who else has a motive?'

'Without knowing precisely how things are currently left, I can't be sure,' Linus said. 'Under her old arrangement, the only other person still alive who would benefit is a Mrs Chilton-Foliat, who bred one of Mrs Egremont's dogs. For all I know, she may have bred more than one of them. She would have stood to get the dogs back and a share of the estate, though with the other breeders all dead, too, I think she'd have got the lot.'

'As good a motive as yours.'

'Yes, but I can't see what opportunity she'd have had. In any case, the will's been changed. There may no longer be any provision for her. There certainly isn't the same provision.'

'Does she know that?'

'How should I know? Mrs Egremont said she hadn't told anyone but once she's found out that her son-in-law knew about it, she might have decided there was no more point in secrecy. No. Wait a minute. That won't wash.'

'Why not?'

'Because if she was exhibiting the symptoms of poison before I saw her last, Mrs Chilton-Foliat wouldn't know she'd changed her will. If the poisoning had started after she'd told her, then she wouldn't have been ill when I was with her.'

'Aren't you forgetting something, Mr Rintoul?'

'Am I? What?'

'It seems likely that only if Mrs Chilton-Foliat *doesn't* know about the change that there's a good motive for her to poison Mrs Egremont and poison is traditionally regarded as a woman's weapon.'

'If she has a motive for disposing of Mrs Egremont, then she has one for getting rid of all the other breeders who stood in the way. Frankly, I can't see her bludgeoning Mrs Flatford to death or tampering with Julian Treorchy's car, and I don't think there's any doubt about who killed poor Sharon Dedham.'

If this was the first intimation the Inspector had had of a possible connection between the three other deaths and Mrs Egremont, he hid it well. Linus had the feeling that it wasn't news to him.

Inspector Rievaulx stood up and closed his notebook. Detective-Sergeant Chacombe followed suit a second later so that they reminded Linus of a not-quite-synchronized imitation of Wilson, Keppel and Betty.

'Thank you for your time, Mr Rintoul,' the Inspector said. 'It's been a most interesting interview.'

This was not, Linus knew, the customary police valediction. 'Is that it?' he said. 'Did you just come here for an academic discussion?'

The Inspector looked at his watch. 'Is there any more?'

The gesture was clearly a theatrical one, not an indication of concern with the amount of time still at their disposal—which would be infinite if they harboured any serious suspicions—so much as the mimed equivalent of 'Goodness me, how time does fly.'

'Well, no,' Linus admitted, because there wasn't. 'It just seems so very . . . inconclusive.'

'But then, isn't that exactly what life is, Mr Rintoul?'

'No, Inspector,' Linus said firmly. 'That's just the one thing life isn't.'

A cloud of mild annoyance passed over the Inspector's face. 'Point taken—but I think you know what I mean. Let's just say you've given us food for thought.'

'It's been a two-way transaction,' Linus told him.

He closed the front door behind his visitors and returned to the sitting-room to pour himself a very stiff whisky. Why did a visit from the police always leave him feeling drained and uneasy, even when his conscience was completely clear?

CHAPTER 8

The injustice of being suspected of something which hadn't even entered his head had an effect on Linus far greater than the mere lowering of the spirits which might have been expected. It was more a corrosion of the spirit, a bitterness due to the realization that he was impotent to do anything about it. Even if he could prove, as he was sure he could, that the suspicion was entirely groundless it was no consolation. His bitterness wasn't directed at the police who had only been doing their job, nor would he have felt bitter towards the doctor if he had been the informant, and for the same reason. His bitterness was directed entirely at George Upperby.

There was the possibility that it had been Mrs Egremont herself who had reported the matter. That would make him sad but it would at least have the side effect of making her change her will which would relieve him of any responsibility at all. However, he was disinclined to think it might have been her doing: it was more in Mrs Egremont's style to tackle him herself, even if she confined it to a letter— which would be a very wise precaution if she thought he had been poisoning her.

It was also quite possible that Winifred had contacted the police. If she had, Linus was quite sure it would have been at her husband's instigation. George seemed much more concerned than his wife about the Egremont inheritance being left elsewhere, yet Linus had so far found no hint that he had at any time stood likely to inherit anything on his own account. No one could accuse him of direct self-interest.

What was much more likely, in Linus's estimation, was that George and Winifred, concerned when Mrs Egremont had told them of her plans for her dogs and her fortune at the time she had first rearranged her affairs to take care of them, had decided to exert what influence they could to make her change her mind. He assumed that previously Winifred had been the main, if not the sole, beneficiary. There would have been no particular hurry: Mrs Egremont was old but not frail and there was no one on the scene who could have been regarded as a rival, other than the dogs themselves. There was time to operate on the softly-softly-catchee-monkey principle. Then Linus had hove into view. Looked at dispassionately, Linus couldn't really blame George for regarding him with deep suspicion. Linus had no idea who could be poisoning the old woman. George could be absolved because it wasn't in his or his wife's interest to do so until she had changed her will back in Winifred's favour. On the other hand, it was undeniably in Linus's interest to dispose of her before she did so. He knew such a thought hadn't even entered his head but only he could be sure of that and, looked at from the outside, there was absolutely no one with a better motive.

He couldn't even ring Mrs Egremont to reassure her: if she didn't think it was him, there was no point, and if she did, well, he would say that, wouldn't he? Such thoughts as these chased themselves around in his head during the day and interfered with his sleep at night until he began to wish with a venom that surprised him, that he had never set eyes on the accursed Madeleine because, if it hadn't been for her, he would never have been in Hunstanton. It suited him to disregard the fact, inconvenient to his anger, that she had wanted somewhere much more lively in the first place.

The Trevarricks' Silver Wedding celebrations came as a welcome, if temporary, respite. Linus got almost as much pleasure from choosing a present as from the occasion itself. Linus liked buying presents much more than he liked receiving them, though this was probably because few people really understood his tastes. He recognized that that was a trap it was very easy to fall into, but since he made a point of trying very hard to put himself into the recipient's shoes instead of simply buying something that he would like to be given himself, he thought it was one he usually avoided fairly well. He did experience a brief, unkind, temptation to realize his threat and give the happy couple a 'gondola' for after-dinner mints and enjoyed himself discovering which were the very worst of the cheap plated ones available. It was difficult to decide where to bestow the accolade but he rather thought one that was chrome-plated was probably the worst. It was almost a pity that he liked the Trevarricks too well to inflict it on them and he settled instead on a cut-crystal fruit bowl of superb quality, whose incised pattern spoke eloquently and gracefully of its Polish origins. It was, he decided, both beautiful and useful and had the added merit of not being too obviously presentational. The shop undertook to gift-wrap it, so Linus was able to hand over something which looked superb even before it was opened.

Len Trevarrick was impressed. 'Didn't know you could wrap things like that,' he said. 'Or did the latest girlfriend do it?'

'There isn't one,' Linus said shortly, cheerfully leaving his boss to assume it was therefore his own handiwork.

'It seems almost a pity to open it,' Diana Trevarrick said.

'I'd rather you did—sooner or later,' Linus replied. 'If you don't, I'll have paid a hell of a lot for a cardboard box and some wrapping-paper.

She laughed and took it over to the table where their presents were displayed. Linus watched her with well-concealed anxiety while she opened it, knowing that her reaction was much more important than her husband's. Her delight in the bowl was clearly unfeigned.

'Linus, it's *stunning*,' she said. 'How did you know we both love cut-glass? I suppose Len dropped a hint.'

Her husband disclaimed the credit.

'No, you can't blame him,' Linus said. 'It was all my own work. You nearly got—' He was about to tell her about the 'gondola' when he saw the very object of his distaste sitting elsewhere on the table, not entirely hidden by a biscuit barrel. 'Something altogether else,' he finished lamely.

Len Trevarrick had seen the direction of his glance and smiled. 'I must introduce you to Fiona,' he said. 'She works in Diana's boutique. Pretty girl. Just your sort and I gather she's between boyfriends right now.' He took Linus's elbow and led him to the bar. 'Give this man a drink,' he said before turning back to Linus. 'She gave us one of those things for mints.' He caught the arm of a well-distributed teenager in a short, spangly, pillar-box red dress and bedroom hair. 'Fiona, let me introduce Linus Rintoul. He's a colleague. He collects pictures.'

Fiona, who might, Linus decided, be as old as nineteen though he doubted it, did her best to conceal her dismay at having foisted upon her a man old enough to be her father and then some, and managed a polite smile.

'You're a vet, are you?' she said.

'That's right. I gather you work for Diana.'

'That's right.' She looked at him. 'Can I ask you something?'

'So long as you don't expect an answer,' he said. He hoped the banality sounded jocular but guessed it merely dated him.

'Being a vet must mean you've got access to all those drugs and things.'

This was not quite the sort of question Linus had expected.

'We do use them, yes,' he said cautiously.

She nudged him with a playful elbow. Her arch smile suggested that perhaps she was beginning to revise her opinion of him. 'I bet you're a real goer,' she said.

'I beg your pardon?' Linus had been called many things in his time. A goer wasn't one of them. He wasn't even sure exactly what it meant but instinct led him to fear the worst.

'You *know*,' she said. 'All those drugs and things. You must be on a high most of the time. Not,' she added thoughtfully, 'that you look as if you're on one now.'

Linus decided this was not a conversation—or an acquaintance—he had any desire to pursue. He took refuge in a po-faced puritanism. 'You're barking up the wrong tree,' he said. 'Wrong sort of drugs and definitely not my

style. And if you've got any sense at all, young lady, it
won't be your style, either.'

'Oh God,' she said disgustedly. 'You're as dire as you
look,' and wasted no more time before prowling in search
of more promising pastures.

Len Trevarrick appeared at Linus's elbow again.
'Doesn't look as if you made a hit there, old man.'

'Good. Mind you, I could have if I'd really tried. All it
needed was a quick snorter of something. I don't know
what she thinks we carry in our little black bags, but I
don't think she's ever heard of Euthobarb. Or maybe it
was just the needles she was after.'

Trevarrick grimaced. 'There's a lot of it about. To be
honest, Linus, these last few weeks you've been looking as
if you could do with a pick-me-up yourself—and I'm not
obliquely offering you illegal substances, or even a quick
whiff of ether. You look as if things are getting on top of
you. Is everything OK?'

'Everything's fine.'

Trevarrick looked at him in silence for a few minutes.
'You never were a good liar,' he said affably. 'Never mind.
Knock a few back and do a bit of mingling. That'll take
your mind off it, whatever it is, even if it's only for tonight.'

It was sound advice and Linus followed it, helped by the
fact that the majority of guests belonged to his generation
and not Fiona's. It was also helped by the fact that not all
the guests were couples and Linus made unashamed use of
the social currency bestowed on him by virtue of nothing
more than his gender and his marital status. A past master
at detecting the glint of the hunter in the eye of unattached,
not-precisely-young females, he none the less enjoyed himself much more than he had anticipated and fell into bed
that night in a tired but cheerful frame of mind of the
sort that had eluded him ever since Detective-Inspector
Rievaulx's visit.

*

The sense of improved well-being lasted for several days, until Mrs Egremont rang him. Linus resisted with difficulty the temptation to hang up at once. Even at once would have been too late: the sound of her voice was enough to puncture his spirits.

'Linus? I'm sorry to be such a nuisance but then I thought, what are friends for it you can't ring them? So I decided to take the bull by the horns. Linus, I'm worried.'

'How are you?' Linus asked. 'Did you go to the doctor after all?'

'The doctor? Oh, that. Yes, I took your advice and that's all sorted out now, thank goodness. I'm fine. Quite recovered. It was rather amusing, as a matter of fact, but that's not why I'm ringing.'

Gob-smacked was the word that sprang to Linus's mind. Rather amusing? Systematic arsenical poisoning? Mrs Egremont had some funny ideas but that was odder than most.

'You didn't seem to be finding it amusing at the time,' he said, unwilling to let her know he had been told about the poisoning because, if it hadn't been she who told the police, she would ask how he knew. 'What did it turn out to be?'

'Would you believe I was being poisoned with arsenic? Small doses every single day? What do you make of that?'

'I certainly don't think it's funny. Are you sure?'

'The doctor was. Thank goodness he's an old man. He said himself he didn't think a younger practitioner would have put two and two together. As it was, he had his suspicions and the labs came up with the verification.'

'You sound remarkably calm about it,' Linus said. 'Did they decide who was responsible?'

'I nearly died laughing when they'd got it all sorted out —only a few days ago, as a matter of fact. It seems it was William.'

'William? Do you mean your husband?' It was the only William Linus had ever heard her mention.

'That's right.'

'But he's dead.'

'I know, and the really comical thing is that he probably killed himself the same way. Inadvertently, of course. They did discuss exhumation but since foul play doesn't enter into it, they're leaving well alone. I'm glad. Exhumation would have been quite unnecessary except as an academic exercise.'

'I'm afraid you've lost me. How could he have inadvertently poisoned himself and then tried systematically to murder you from the grave? This is late-night horror movie stuff, not real life.'

'It's also high farce. The poisoning started from the moment I slept in his room. Do you remember that room?'

'I found it dark and depressing.'

'Do you recall the wallpaper.'

Linus cast his mind back. 'It was green, I think. Not, in my opinion, a particularly attractive shade. Wasn't it part of a batch he'd brought back from somewhere?'

'That's right. It was antique. One of the joys of his life, he used to say.' She chuckled. 'Serve him right, too. If he'd been content with a nice little regency-stripe from Do-It-All he might still be alive today.'

'I'm still mystified,' Linus told her.

'It's quite simple. That green was very fashionable at one time. They call the colour "Paris green", apparently. Anyway, it seems that particular shade is achieved by the use of arsenic. That wallpaper is hand-painted. That added to its value, of course. As it aged, the paint began to flake off, a process which was aggravated by getting it off its original wall, rolling it up and transporting it here. I dare say you may have noticed the damaged bits. I've been guilty myself of rubbing my hand over any bit that seemed powdery and I expect William did the same: it's like pulling the hairs out of a moulting dog—you can't resist the temptation to go on doing it—it's irresistible, especially when pulling one out loosens another. Anyway, the upshot was that anyone breathing in that room would be inhaling small particles of arsenic and by sleeping there, one was breathing in quite a lot of it.'

'Good God,' Linus said. 'And that's the explanation? I take it you've redecorated the room?'

'Straight away. The good thing about it was that even Winifred couldn't argue against it any more.'

Linus pricked up his ears. 'So Winifred and her husband have only just learned about it?'

'I told you, they only discovered the source of the poisoning a few days ago.'

'Was that the first they heard about it?'

'No. I'm really rather ashamed of myself: when Dr Knottingley confirmed that I was being poisoned, I did rather let rip into George. I told him he ought to be bright enough to realize that he would be cutting off his nose to spite his face if he poisoned me, because once I was dead, I'd be in no position to change things back in favour of Winifred. He was very angry indeed and said he certainly wasn't that stupid and that I should look elsewhere. He was implying that it was you, of course, but I knew you better than that and I've been proved right.'

'True, but it means his anger was entirely justified.'

'I know, and I ought to apologize but I don't think I will. He's an odious man. And that's why I'm ringing you.'

'You'd better explain,' Linus told her, unable to think of anything he could add to her assessment of her son-in-law's character.

'It's Winifred. She's missing. She disappeared soon after I told them about the wallpaper. It seems she went shopping and simply didn't come back.'

'What do the police say?'

'That's just it. George refuses to call them. He says give

her time and she'll be back. I'm not so sure. It's so out of character. I think he knows more than he's admitting,' she added darkly.

'Quite possibly he does,' Linus replied. 'But if you're trying to imply that he's done away with her, I think you're on the wrong tack.'

'Do you? I didn't think you liked George.'

'I don't but I can't see what my personal feelings have got to do with it. People don't do away with other people without a very good reason and one of the best motives ever invented is financial gain. Now if Winifred dies before you, George can't benefit from anything she might otherwise have inherited—unless, of course, you've made provision for him to do so.'

'Certainly not,' Mrs Egremont said firmly. 'Why should I? He's not a blood relation.'

'Neither am I,' Linus pointed out.

'That's different. But what do I do for the best, Linus? I'm worried about her and I think the police *should* be told, don't you?'

'To be perfectly honest, I think George has to be the best judge of that. After all, he is her husband, he's the one who knows what sort of a mood she was in, what relations between them were like. For all you or I know, she might have had a fancy man on the side. Maybe she's gone off with him. It could be that George knows all about it but doesn't want to upset you by telling you in the hope that she'll soon be back and no one but themselves need ever know.'

'Spare my feelings?' Mrs Egremont said scornfully. 'The thought never entered his head. More likely his own pride wouldn't let him admit it. Loss of face and all that.'

'Equally likely,' Linus agreed. 'Doesn't alter the basic premise, does it?'

'I suppose not,' she admitted grudgingly. Her tone brightened. 'You don't think he might have killed her out of jealousy? It's a motive every bit as strong as greed.'

This was undoubtedly true but Linus still couldn't quite see George Upperby locked so firmly in the grip of jealous passion that he would kill his wife—or even her lover. He could, however, see him keeping quiet about it in order to save face, hoping that it would all sort itself out with none but the participants any the wiser.

'I still think it isn't very likely,' he said. 'How long has she been gone? Exactly, I mean. Is it days or weeks?'

'Days. Three—no, four. If George is telling me the truth, that is. I spoke to her five days ago about redecorating William's room and George says she went the day after.'

'If you spoke to her five days ago you know George can't be far out. I see no reason to doubt him. As for going to the police, I don't think they'd take much notice of either of you until she's been gone a week or so, and they really will take more notice of George. You'll just have to persuade him. If he won't do anything after, say, ten days, I think you'd be justified in going to them if you still can't persuade George to.'

'You really think it's too soon?'

'Yes, I do.'

Mrs Egremont sounded unconvinced. 'I suppose I could wait a little longer but it goes against my instincts.'

'I'm sure it does and my sympathies are with you. The police will work on the knowledge that most people reported missing turn up within a few days, usually with an entirely rational explanation for their disappearance.'

'I'll leave it, then,' she said, though she still sounded doubtful. 'I trust your advice but in this instance it won't be easy.'

'It might help to remind yourself that if she's been gone four days already, you've only got another three to wait.'

'It might,' Mrs Egremont said sharply, and hung up.

*

It was only two days later that Linus was recalled to the office by means of a message left at the deer-farm he was inspecting. The farm secretary was quite adamant that he was to return at once. 'They said something had cropped up and you were to drop everything and run. I don't think they meant the last bit literally,' she added helpfully.

'No hint what it was about?'

'No. I did ask but they muttered something about professional ethics.'

'Mine or theirs?'

She shrugged. 'They didn't say.'

Linus drove back to the city casting about in his mind to discover in what way he might have transgressed. He could think of nothing and finally decided the phrase must just have been MAFF's way of shutting up an inquisitive outsider.

Two men rose to their feet as he entered his office. This time he recognized them at once. Detective-Inspector Rievaulx and Detective-Sergeant Chacombe.

'Good afternoon, Mr Rintoul.'

'It was, Inspector. What's so urgent that I have to be called away from an inspection?'

'I wonder if you'd be kind enough to accompany us to the police station. We think you may be able to help us with our inquiries.'

'Into what?'

'All in good time, Mr Rintoul—and I don't think your place of work is the best place to ask questions, do you?'

'Which police station?'

'The main one. St Aldate's.'

Linus led the way but instead of going straight down the corridor he stepped through the open doorway of the secretarial office. He took a ballpoint from the lilac plastic desk-tidy and scribbled a name and a telephone number on to a jotter. Then he tore off the page and handed it to the secretary. 'Lisa, this is my solicitor. Please phone my home number tonight at, let's see—' and he consulted his watch—'at nine o'clock and if I'm not there, ring him and tell him I was taken to St Aldate's. I haven't a clue why but I've a hunch I may need him. OK?'

Her eyes widened and she looked from him to his escort and back. 'Yes, of course, Mr Rintoul,' she said with unaccustomed formality, and slipped the piece of paper into her handbag.

Linus was disconcerted to discover that the interview was to be recorded: it lent a Big Brother air to the exercise even though his common sense told him it was probably in his own interests.

'If this is about Mrs Egremont,' he began, 'I think you're on the wrong tack—or haven't you been told that the source of her arsenical poisoning has been found?'

'We are aware of that, yes, but why should you assume it's in connection with that that we wish to talk to you?' the Inspector asked.

Linus stared at him, puzzled. 'What else could it be? She's the only conceivable connection between me and Norfolk, which is your bailiwick.'

'Is she?'

'You know she is.' Something in the policeman's manner sowed a small seed of doubt. 'Isn't she?'

'I believe you're acquainted with other people resident within what you choose to call my bailiwick.'

'Am I? Well, yes, if you mean the Upperbys—but the word is "acquainted"; I wouldn't claim to know them.'

'I wonder whether your definition of the difference between knowing someone and merely being acquainted with them would be the same as mine? Let's see if we have the same ideas. How well do you know Winifred Upperby, Mrs Egremont's daughter?'

'Hardly at all. Less well than her husband, as a matter of fact. He's gone out of his way to be singularly obnoxious,

so I've had a chance to form a more definite opinion about
him.' Light began to dawn. 'Oh, I see what you're after. I
take it Winifred hasn't turned up yet? Tell me, was it Mrs
Egremont who told you she was missing or did she finally
persuade George to report it?'

'So you knew she was missing. How did you come by
that information?'

'Mrs Egremont rang me. She was very concerned and
wanted to know what she should do.'

'What did you tell her?'

'She wanted to call your lot but Winifred had only been
gone four days and I suggested she should wait until a week
had passed.'

'Why did you think that was a good idea?'

'Because I've gathered that the police aren't too much
bothered about a missing adult for the first few days since,
if they're not handicapped and are in good health, there's
a good chance they'll turn up again, anyway.'

'And from whom have you "gathered" this?'

Linus thought about it. 'I don't know,' he said finally.
'I suppose it's the message that's got across from countless
television programmes.'

'Do you always form your opinions on the basis of what
you've seen on the telly, Mr Rintoul? I must say, you've
always struck me as a more intelligent man than that.'

'No, of course I don't, but missing people isn't something
I've ever sat down and thought about and it's not something I've ever come up against in my everyday life. If
I've seen anything about it on TV, it's been in a fictional
programme.'

'And there was no other reason for telling her to wait?'

'Advising, not telling. But no, there was no other reason.'

'So when did you last see Winifred Upperby?'

'God knows. I can recall the occasion but I'd have to
look the date up in my diary. I'd taken Mrs Egremont to
visit a friend in hospital in Shrewsbury. Ted Blandford.

The Upperbys were waiting at Mrs Egremont's house when we got back.'

'Was it a friendly meeting?'

'Not particularly. Certainly not where George Upperby was concerned. He felt I was a con-man moving in on his mother-in-law in expectation of good pickings once she was dead.'

'A reasonable expectation, as I understand.'

'So I'm told. And I have to admit that I can't altogether blame Upperby for his suspicions: they're unfounded, but in his shoes I'd feel just the same.'

'What were his wife's feelings on the subject?'

'I don't know. Probably not very different, I suppose, but she was much more restrained, better mannered. She gave no indication of her feelings on the subject.'

'Not even privately?'

'How should I know what she said privately?'

'She didn't ever talk to you about it when you were alone?'

'If she had, I'd have known her views, wouldn't I?' Linus pointed out reasonably. 'In any case, I can't recall an occasion when we ever were alone.'

'What, none? Ever?'

Linus thought about it. 'I don't think so. No.'

'Are you aware that her husband believes she had a lover?'

'No. He didn't exactly come to me to unburden his soul, Inspector.'

'Do you think she had one?'

'I've no idea. I told you, I scarcely knew the woman.'

'Yet it was a possibility you mentioned to her mother.'

'Did I? Oh yes, I remember: I said that maybe she'd gone off with a fancy man. It wasn't because I necessarily thought that was the explanation but because it was a far less worrying one to put into Mrs Egremont's mind than the alternative that was obviously bothering the old lady.'

'Which was what?'

'That Winifred had been attacked, possibly killed.'

The Inspector looked at him thoughtfully. 'You're an intelligent man, Mr Rintoul, and an educated one. Are you given to what one might call a serpentine habit of thought?'

'I'm not devious, if that's what you mean.'

'Not quite. Let me put it another way: do you sometimes take refuge in semantics?'   ·

Linus chuckled. 'It has been known—especially when I'm dealing with someone who wants to pin me down.'

'That was my information. Also that you have a rather irritating, Jesuitical habit of choosing a pattern of words that enables you to tell the truth in such a way that the listener infers the precise opposite.'

'Now there I take issue with you, Inspector. I really can't accept responsibility for what others choose to infer. They should listen to the words. Not jump to conclusions.'

'Sound advice, Mr Rintoul. I'll bear it in mind.'

Linus sighed.'Inspector, I'm making every effort to be helpful.'

'I'm glad to hear it, especially since anything else could lay you open to a charge of obstructing the police. How long had you and Mrs Upperby been lovers?'

'How long . . . ? What are you talking about? We weren't!'

'No? Or isn't that just what you would say, given the circumstances?'

'Given the circumstances that we weren't, yes. Good God, man, the thought never crossed my mind! Winifred Upperby isn't my cup of tea *at all*.'

'You go for bimbos, do you?'

Linus thought of Fiona and shuddered. 'No, I do not. There's quite a wide range of women in between those two extremes, you know.'

'You rate Winifred Upperby an extreme, do you?'

Linus thought about it briefly. 'Yes, I suppose I do. She

strikes me as being very conventional, rather worthy, probably reasonably bright, very self-controlled—and not very interesting. I should think I'd find it difficult to discover any interest we might have in common. She doesn't appeal, Inspector. I like a woman with a bit of élan, if you know what I mean. I can't honestly say I've ever noticed any of that in Mrs Upperby. In fact, now you mention it, I'm not sure I can envisage her in the marital bed, much less someone else's.'

'You know the old adage about still waters?'

'There's always that,' Linus conceded. 'In her case I'd be inclined to say still and turgid.'

'I don't suppose you can remember where you were on the evening of the twenty-third? Last Saturday?'

'I was at my boss's Silver Wedding party.'

'Where was that held? At an hotel?'

'No, at their house. Do you want their address?'

'If you wouldn't mind.' Linus gave it to him. Inspector Rievaulx continued, 'When did you get there?'

'I didn't look at my watch so I can't be sure, but I can work out a rough figure.'

'Do your best.'

'The invitation was for seven-thirty but my wife trained me well. She made it clear that the last thing one ever did at that sort of function was to arrive on time. So I didn't but, since I'm obsessively punctual I can never bring myself to be very late. I may have got there by eight but I think it was more likely at quarter past. I wasn't the first—nor was I the last by any means.'

'Big party, was it?'

'What used to be called a sad crush, Inspector. I don't know how many guests there were but we were pretty tightly packed.'

'Did you go alone?'

'Yes.'

'Had you arranged to meet anyone there?'

'No.'

'I don't suppose you spoke to your host or hostess while you were there?'

Linus stared at him. 'What do you take me for?' he demanded. 'How can you go to a party at someone's house and not speak to the people giving it?'

'You'd be surprised.'

'Not me. I gave them their present. We spoke.'

'Did you know any of the other guests?'

'Some of them.'

'Who else did you speak to?'

'Apart from people I knew? A number of unattached women, as it happens, starting with a real bimbo called Fiona.'

'Fiona what?'

'No idea. Diana Trevarrick will know—she works in Diana's boutique. We chatted for a while but separated by mutual consent when I discovered she thought being a vet meant I had all sorts of interesting drugs in my bag and she discovered I didn't.'

'And the others?'

Linus gave him some names. 'You'll have to ask Diana for any details. They were pleasant enough to chat to at that sort of do but none whose acquaintance I wanted to pursue.'

'Not enough élan?'

Linus laughed. 'You could say that.'

'Did you leave with any of them?'

'I've told you, I didn't want to pursue their acquaintance.'

'Does that mean no?'

'Yes, Inspector, it means no.'

'So when did you leave?'

Linus frowned. 'I don't know. Late. After midnight. At a guess, I'd say between one and two. I did take my leave of Len and Diana but whether they'd remember the time would be rather doubtful, I should think, in the circumstances.'

'And you drove home?'

'No, I took a taxi.' Linus frowned. 'I haven't a clue which firm it was.'

'You can't think of anything else that would pin down the time you got home?'

'No—yes. I'd had quite a bit to drink and I tripped getting out of the taxi and swore. The chap next door stuck his head out of the window and kicked up a fuss. He'll remember the time.'

'Have you any recollection of leaving the party between the time you arrived and the time you went home?'

'I wasn't *that* drunk. No, I was there all the time.'

'Thank you, Mr Rintoul. We shall have to check this out but it sounds as if you're in the clear.'

'In the clear for what?'

'The murder of Winifred Upperby. Haven't you seen it in the papers?'

'No. Are you allowed to tell me any more?'

Inspector Rievaulx hesitated and then said, 'I can tell you what's public knowledge. She was found in the woods around Grimes Graves. She hadn't put up a struggle and she had had sexual intercourse, so we're inclined to think that her husband's suspicion that she had a lover might be accurate.'

'And he gave you my name?'

'We had come across you before, Mr Rintoul.'

'I'd have thought it would be rather difficult to sustain an affair when one of you lived in Oxford and the other in Norfolk,' Linus said.

'But not impossible. Now perhaps you'd like some food sent up from the canteen.'

'I'd rather go home.'

'I'm sure you would. Bear with us, Mr Rintoul. We have to check your statements out first. That will take some time but if they support your version, we'll send you home.'

'You want to get to any witnesses first, I take it.'

'Of course.'

Several tedious hours passed before Linus was driven home, completely exonerated from any part in Winifred's death. Linus suspected that he had good cause to be glad he had made a point of circulating among the unattached women at the Trevarricks' bash: it meant that they had remembered him and, even though their testimony couldn't possibly have accounted for every minute of the anniversary celebrations, it would have been enough to preclude his getting to Norfolk and back.

He poured himself a drink and sank back on to the sofa, his feet on the coffee table. What now? He supposed that he ought to ring Mrs Egremont to offer his condolences on her daughter's death, though he would have preferred to be shot of the whole business. It began to look as if his almost flippant remark about Winifred's having a lover had been all too close to the truth, improbable as it seemed. Who would have thought Winifred had it in her? In that case, it was equally possible that George had acted out of jealousy but if so, what had happened to the lover? Had he run off, ignominiously leaving Winifred to her fate or had George been more successful in hiding a second body? Those were questions which would occur to the police without any prompting from Linus. His great consolation was that, since this could not, by any stretch of the imagination, be attributed to Mrs Egremont's successive will changes, at least he needn't feel guilty. It was a pity that Winifred's death meant that it was even more unlikely that he would be able to persuade Mrs Egremont to leave her money elsewhere, because he thought she would rate the impersonal nature of a charity less highly than her judgement of an individual's sense of duty and, with Winifred dead,

George could have no further interest in what happened to her estate.

Since the police would certainly take George in for questioning and would be likely to keep him in for a long time, even if they ultimately released him, Mrs Egremont would be in even greater need of someone with a shoulder on which to lean. Linus looked at his watch. It was a symbolic gesture because he knew she would still be in bed. He'd be better off there himself, if it came to that. He'd go up now and wake up when he woke up and to hell with MAFF. If the hour was relatively civilized when he came to, he'd ring her then.

Mrs Egremont was almost pathetically glad to hear his voice. 'Are you all right, Linus? Have the police been questioning you?' she asked.

'Yes on both counts,' Linus told her. 'They've released me because I've got a perfect alibi, thank goodness: I was at my boss's Silver Wedding party and several of the other guests remember me at intervals through the evening, so I gather that lets me off the hook. More importantly, how are you?'

'There's nothing wrong with my health, but my nerves are all to pieces. They're questioning George, of course, and there doesn't seem to be anyone I can turn to. The Chilton-Foliats have been very helpful but it's not the same: I don't really rate them as friends.'

'Perhaps you should,' Linus said gently. 'At times like this it's the people that rally round that are your real friends.'

'I suppose so.' She sounded doubtful. 'Linus, if it wouldn't be too great an imposition, I'd like you to come to the funeral with me. They're releasing the body tomorrow.'

'I'd be happy to,' Linus lied. It wasn't a request he'd anticipated, having assumed, in so far as he'd given it any thought at all, that either the funeral had already taken place or the police were hanging on to the body until their investigations were complete.

'No, you won't,' Mrs Egremont said shrewdly, with a return to something like her usual acerbity. 'You'd rather be almost anywhere else but attending funerals isn't a thing most people have the nerve to back out of.'

Linus chuckled. 'No one can accuse you of being ga-ga,' he commented.

'I should hope not!' she retorted. 'It's very much to your credit that you're prepared to put yourself out for the sake of an old woman's feelings.'

'As long as you don't think it's for the old woman's money.'

'This is me you're talking to, not George,' she said sharply. 'They're letting him come to the funeral—under escort, I expect. I'd rather he weren't there.'

'Winifred was his wife,' Linus pointed out, 'and if he hasn't been charged there's still the possibility he wasn't the one who killed her, in which case, whatever you may think of him, it would be a cruelty not to allow him to be there.'

'Did you know he was the one who put the police on to you? He told them he thought you were Winifred's lover.'

'I guessed as much. It doesn't alter the situation.'

There was a long pause at the other end of the line. 'You're a very good man, Linus Rintoul. Has anyone ever told you that?'

Linus laughed. 'No, I can't say they have. Now when do you want me to come over?'

One did not expect to enjoy a funeral, Linus told himself firmly. That wasn't what they were for. He supposed they were an inevitable concomitant of growing old and the older one became, the more likely one was to be attending the funerals of all those friends who were dying first. Maybe there came a time in one's life when funerals replaced weddings as the major social function. It was an awesome thought.

Mrs Egremont's guess had been quite right: George was present with an escort. It was discreet, plain-clothes and self-effacing, but quite unmistakable. What was rather more surprising was that George was allowed back to the house for the wake. His escort came too, and it crossed Linus's mind that it was an arrangement that must suit Detective-Inspector Rievaulx very well: he had two quiet observers there, making themselves rather more inconspicuous than the wallpaper, in an ideal position for picking up the unconscious hint, the injudicious phrase.

The only people present with whom he was acquainted, other than George, were the Chilton-Foliats, both of whom were being quietly helpful.

'Mrs E. must be quite shattered,' Meriel murmured as she offered him a plate of sandwiches. 'She's lost so many people who were her friends just lately.'

'I think she is,' Linus agreed. 'She hides it well and there's no denying she's a resilient old lady, but it must leave its mark.'

'I think she's quite amazing,' Meriel agreed.

Conversation was at the level, only slightly above a murmur, which is customary at such affairs in England and reminded Linus of that which takes place among a stage-crowd where one hears the murmur but not the words. It was a convention with which everyone was familiar, including George Upperby, who broke it.

'That's the one you've got to watch,' he told Charles Chilton-Foliat who happened to be standing quite close to him. 'That's the snake in the grass who's conning my mother-in-law out of all she owns,' and he nodded in Linus's direction.

'Steady, now,' one of his escort said.

'Don't you "steady now" me,' George retorted. 'That vet, the one who's been oh-so-nice to a little old lady, has already conned her into changing her will in his favour. Winifred had something coming to her but now he gets it all. You can draw your own conclusions even if it's beyond the police's powers to put two and two together.'

'Think you've got it wrong, old chap,' Charles Chilton-Foliat protested. 'Your mother told me it was being shared between the people who bred her dogs.'

'Oh, it was, it was,' George said. 'Only after she met this Rintoul, she went out and changed it all. She didn't let you all know that, though, did she? It was only by sheer good luck we learned about it. The first arrangement was bad enough in my book, but the current one ... And would you believe he has the gall to pretend he doesn't want it?'

The room fell silent, those not actively involved in this little altercation studiously admiring the view, the pictures or the refreshments—anything to distance themselves from what was going on without distancing them so much that they wouldn't be able to hear it.

Linus was too angry to dare to speak but Mrs Egremont had no such inhibitions. She strode across the room and slapped her son-in-law smartly across the face.

'I'm not fooled by you, George Upperby. I never have been. For all your protestations of not needing my money, you still couldn't face the prospect of it going to someone else. You knew that if it went to Winifred, you'd be able to wheedle—con might be a better word—most of it away from her on one pretext or another even though the two of you had more than enough to live on comfortably for evermore. Linus has never, ever, put any pressure on me. His advice right from the beginning was to leave it to a canine charity and let them administer it. He didn't even know about the change until after it was made and then he objected very strongly.'

'Oh yes?' George sneered. 'A case of "the lady doth protest too much", was it?'

'No,' Linus said. He felt he had himself under sufficient

control now to take part. 'If I can persuade your mother-in-law to leave it elsewhere, believe me, I shall. But I'd be lying if I pretended I'd do anything other than dissuade her from including you in her bequests.'

'Don't worry,' Mrs Egremont interrupted. 'There's no chance of that.' She turned to the policeman. 'You can take this man away with you. Now.' She turned back to her son-in-law. 'Get out, George, and if some idiot policeman ever lets you out of custody, don't bother to come back here. I want nothing more to do with you. I don't want to see your face ever again. Take him away.' She turned her back to emphasize her point and, after a brief, embarrassed pause, the two plain-clothes men took George Upperby by the arm and gently propelled him through the silent guests to the front door. As the sound of the police car's wheels crunching on the gravel announced their departure, Mrs Egremont turned back to her guests.

'I'm sorry about that little scene,' she said. 'I'm very upset by Winifred's death and I'm very tired. I'd like to lie down so I'd be very grateful if you'd all go home. Thank you for coming.'

Cups and saucers were put down and the mourners took their leave with what Linus could only call quiet expedition: they appeared not to make undue haste yet the house was soon empty of everyone except himself, Mrs Egremont and the Chilton-Foliats.

'We'll help you clear up,' Meriel offered.

'I'll do that,' Linus said. 'I'm sure Mrs Egremont will be grateful for your help when I've gone. I live too far away to keep popping over and I'm sure she'll appreciate friends who live so much closer.'

'Right you are,' Charles Chilton-Foliat said. 'We'll have you to it. One of us will ring you from time to time, Maud, to see how you're doing and if there's anything we can do, just pick up the phone.'

Mrs Egremont thanked them and Linus saw them out.

When he returned, Mrs Egremont was sitting in the fireside chair. 'Silly man,' she said. 'As if picking up the phone would be any use. Doesn't he know you have to dial?'

'You know perfectly well that's what he meant,' Linus said. 'Now I suggest you do exactly what you told them all you were going to do—go to bed.'

'That was only to get rid of them.'

'I know it was. It was a good idea, all the same. You go to bed while I clear this lot away and wash up.'

'And then you'll be off home?'

Linus would have liked to say yes, but he guessed that sleep was what she was most in need of just now and she was unlikely to let herself drop off if she was waiting to say goodbye to him. 'No, I'll book in to the hotel I usually use and I'll be off in the morning. I'll come round and make sure you're all right first, though. Now go to bed and leave me to get on with it.'

She did as she was told and Linus discovered that there is nothing like a large pile of washing-up to occupy the hands while the mind is free to thrash out all sorts of problems. By the time he had finished, he had a fair idea of what he was going to do. It wouldn't hurt to sleep on it, though, and see if it still seemed like a good idea in the morning.

CHAPTER 9

Linus had decided to wait until he put his scheme into operation because he didn't want it to appear to be something arrived at on the spur of the moment or in a fit of pique. The waiting wasn't easy. He wanted the whole matter settled and any delay was an irritation. As a consequence of this, his planned week's delay shrank to four days. On the fourth day, therefore, he wrote Mrs Egremont a letter in which he hoped he struck a nice balance between firmness and diplomacy. His message was simple: he urged her to reconsider the terms of her will because, as things stood, he would feel obliged to refuse to accept both the responsibilities she intended laying upon him and any personal bequests she might have made; he repeated his advice as to a more appropriate beneficiary but added that the decision was entirely hers and he hoped she would do what she saw fit without reference to any views he might hold.

He had hoped that might be the end of it but he wasn't altogether surprised to get a telephone call from her. She was upset—and not only about his letter.

The police had released George Upperby without charging him.

'Perhaps he didn't do it,' Linus suggested. 'He must have been able to offer an alibi.'

'And do you know what it was?' she demanded.

'Of course I don't.'

'He'd been at a meeting of his Masonic lodge!'

'I should think that constituted a cast-iron alibi.'

'Exactly. They all gave statements that he'd been there the whole time.'

'Then why are you so angry? Presumably he was. Or did you *want* him to be guilty?'

'Who else could it have been?'

'The unidentified lover, perhaps?'

'A jealous husband is a much more likely candidate.'

'I think you have to be reasonable about this: I agree that George would appear to have the best motive but if he's been cleared, then that's that. You may not like it but I think you just have to accept it.'

'Cleared!' she snorted. 'And by whom? By a bunch of fellow Masons. What confidence can you place in that?'

'They can't all be liars—or at least, they won't all be willing to perjure themselves.'

'No? Well, I suppose they won't need to, will they? I

mean, I dare say the police are only too happy to have such an easy let-out for one of their own.'

'Now you're just being paranoid about this whole Masonry business,' Linus told her. 'Is that what you rang me about?'

'In part—and I feel better now I've said it to *someone*, even if it turns out to be someone who thinks I'm daft.'

'I didn't say that and I don't think it. Just a bit over-wrought at the moment, and no one can blame you for that.'

'It's this letter of yours, Linus. That's what's upset me. You took a great deal of care over the wording of it, didn't you?'

'Does it show?' he said ruefully. 'Yes, I did. I knew you wouldn't like it so I phrased it as tactfully as I could but I meant every word of it.'

'I realized that but I'm not happy about it. Linus, I'd like us to talk about it. Not now, not on the phone, but face to face.'

'Is there much point?' Linus asked. She was proposing the one thing he had hoped to avoid.

'Please, Linus—it's the least you can do for an old lady.' It was rampant emotional blackmail and they both knew it.

Linus sighed. If it would shift the whole business on to someone else's shoulders—and that was his unashamedly selfish goal—it might be worth the effort, and if he was going to make the effort then the sooner, the better.

'I could manage Sunday afternoon,' he said without any alacrity.

'Not a weekend,' she replied. 'Too many people about.'

'What about the next weekend?' Linus suggested, assuming she meant she had house-guests.

'Every weekend is crowded. Well, not *crowded* perhaps, but even half a dozen people is too many. There's almost never anybody there on a weekday evening. The place is locked up and it's all deserted.'

Linus, who had assumed he would be going to her house, was puzzled. 'I think we're at cross purposes,' he said. 'Had you somewhere in mind other than your house?'

'Didn't I say? I miss Winifred, you know, even though I didn't see her as often as I'd have liked because of that awful husband of hers. I drive out to the woods where she was found sometimes and just sit there. It's very peaceful, very . . . calming. I thought, if we agreed to meet in the evening, you wouldn't have to take a whole day off work. You'd need to leave a bit early, but you could get there by seven or half-past. What do you think?'

It would certainly be more convenient and had the merit of rendering it impossible for the meeting to last too long. Linus reached for his diary. 'It'll need to be the end of the week,' he said. 'Let's say Friday.'

Mrs Egremont hesitated. 'I'm supposed to be going to the Chilton-Foliats' for supper. They've been very good to me, Linus—you were right, they've proved themselves real friends. Still, I don't suppose they'll be too upset if I cancel just this once. I'm sure they'll understand.'

'Friday it is, then. Now how do I find this place. If it's woods, we could be wandering round for hours looking for each other.'

'Did you ever go to Grimes Graves when you were here?'

'No. I've seen them on the map, though.'

'They're in wide-open heathland but it's surrounded by woods. I suggest we meet in the car park there. It isn't the sort that can be closed when the place itself is locked up. Shall we say quarter past seven?'

'I can't guarantee to be there on the dot,' Linus warned. 'Not at the end of a good three hours of motoring.'

'If you're not there by eight, I'll go on home.'

'It doesn't sound like the sort of place you ought to be hanging around on your own,' Linus said doubtfully.

'Nonsense. I shall shut myself up in the car and if it will make you feel happier about it, I'll dig out William's old shotgun and take that along with me. It hasn't got any ammunition but I think it will have a sufficiently deterrent effect, especially in the hands of a little old lady who just might hit the target by accident.'

Linus resolved to be on time. 'As long as you don't wave it in my direction,' he said and they both laughed.

It was close upon half past seven when Linus drove along the rough track, edged with conifers, that led to Grimes Graves. When he had made the arrangement with Mrs Egremont he had forgotten to make allowances for the shortening days. He could see the Armstrong-Siddeley neatly parked in the car park ahead of him, though from this distance there was no sign of its occupant.

He backed his own car into place beside the other and caught a glimpse through the trees on the far side of the site of another car almost, but not quite, completely hidden from view. A fence divided the surrounding forest from the archæological site itself, so it must have got there by a quite different route. Probably a courting couple, Linus thought. So much for Mrs Egremont's total privacy. He wondered briefly whether that was where Winifred and her putative lover used to meet.

When he climbed out of his car, the full force of the wind that blew across the wide expanse of open heath hit him and he leaned back inside for his Barbour. It wasn't raining and didn't look as if it would but it kept the wind out, too. He shrugged himself into the jacket and locked the car and then, as an afterthought, got his torch out of the boot and slipped it into the capacious waxed pocket. It was a long way from dark yet but if Mrs Egremont intended to go into the woods, the light would be gone much more quickly and Linus liked to be sure of finding his way back.

But where was Mrs Egremont? There was no sign of her

in the car which is where she had said she'd be, though he could see on the back seat the shotgun to which she had referred. Obviously she hadn't been joking.

He looked around, half expecting to see her sprawled among the hundreds of green craters that were the only remaining outward signs of the neolithic flint-mining complex that lay beneath his feet. It was the sort of surface that would be treacherous to anyone not entirely steady on his feet. A woman in her eighties might well come a cropper in this sort of landscape.

But there was nothing, no one. He heard the raucous cry of a cock pheasant from the woods but apart from the two cars and himself, the only signs of modern man were a Portakabin a few yards away and a smaller, equally uninspired, building beyond it. From this distance he guessed that the bigger of the two was the entrance to the Graves and the smaller was probably a ventilation shaft. Perhaps Mrs Egremont was sheltering from the wind behind one or other structure, though why she should have chosen that in preference to sitting in a snug car escaped him.

The bigger and nearer of the two structures proved to be the visitors' centre and not, so far as Linus could deduce from peering through the windows, the entrance to any of the shafts. Mrs Egremont was not sheltering in its lee, nor could he see any sign of her inside and, since the doors were firmly locked, it was unlikely she would be in any of the sections where his view was impeded.

He called her name a few times but since his voice was always carried away by the wind and therefore couldn't be heard by anyone not immediately downwind of him, he soon gave that up.

Then he returned to the Armstrong-Siddeley. Had he missed something? A note on top of the console or left on one of the seats? Nothing.

That left the structure he took to be a ventilation shaft. Was it made in such a way that an elderly person could slip and fall into it? It didn't look like it from here but that was no good reason for not investigating. He strode across the heath, bracing himself against the wind.

It wasn't a ventilation shaft at all but a small glazed cabin protecting the entrance to the mine-shaft from the weather. It was obviously normally locked after opening hours but on this occasion the padlock hung open from its hasp. An envelope had been stuck to the inside of the glass, utilizing a small corner of the flap that had escaped its original sealing-down. A message was written on it in block capitals:

LINUS—INSIDE OUT OF WIND. MAUD E.

Linus frowned. Had she found it open? Had the Ministry of Works—Linus refused to accept that there hadn't been such a thing for decades because he felt it was a far more appropriate name than any of its successors—been careless enough to leave it unsecured? Still, the note was unambiguously intended for him. He opened the door.

There was very little floor space inside, most of the area being taken up with the vertical pit-shaft. A ladder had been secured to one side of it of the sort that has hoops of metal at intervals so that, while one can still loose one's footing and slide to the bottom, it would be difficult to fall —or be pushed—off and break one's neck. It was, Linus thought scornfully, just the sort of namby-pamby safety precaution which was so fashionable nowadays and which not only removed any remote risk of injury but also effectively destroyed any sense at all of what it must have been like to be neolithic man creeping down into the dark to mine his tools. In Linus's eyes the insult was aggravated by the sight of neat yellow safety helmets hanging from pegs in the little entrance booth.

Peering down the shaft, he could, of course see only a dim circle at the bottom since the only light that entered came from the sky above. Within that circle he could make out nothing. It was a good job some instinct had made him bring his torch.

He drew it out of his pocket and switched it on. At the bottom of the shaft was a gallery which, so far as he could make out, was roughly circular and larger than he would have expected. He called down.

'Mrs Egremont!'

No answer.

His voice had seemed to echo down the funnel of the shaft but Linus remembered that Mrs Egremont was deaf and, while she couldn't have failed to hear the sound he made, the acoustics might well have been such that she couldn't possibly make out what he had said or identify the voice. With the door left unlocked it made sense for her to lie low until she was sure. He supposed he'd have to go down himself. It was not a prospect that appealed and he thought bitterly that it would have made a lot more sense had she done what she had originally intended, and stayed in the car.

Linus stepped gingerly on to the top rung. He always felt a slight feeling of panic in a very enclosed space and, though the shaft itself was wide enough not to cause too many problems, the restrictions of the enfolding metal hoops made him breathe that bit faster.

Once his head was below the top, he called out again but there was no reply. He flashed his torch round the ground below him and this time was able to see that there were low, arched alcoves at roughly equal distances apart all round the shaft. Someone was sitting on the chalk floor, leaning against one of the dividing 'pillars' of chalk.

A woman.

A woman who looked remarkably like Mrs Egremont.

Linus called out again and, as the words died away it dawned on him that, although he couldn't quite put his finger on the reason, there was something about the way she was sitting that looked more like a rag doll than a real woman. A real *live* woman, that is.

His dislike of the tunnelled ladder vanished and he completed the descent without further delay.

His fears were realized. The figure was Mrs Egremont and she was very, very dead.

The torch-beam illuminated the dark, coagulated blood that had run down the side of her face on to her shoulder. Linus managed to curb his professional instinct to discover why—it wasn't an action the police would thank him for —but he had very little doubt that, if he had done so, he would have found her head to have been smashed in with something heavy.

The grating sound of an unoiled hinge made him spin round. It took a few seconds before he recognized the figure who must have emerged from an alcove behind him because his attention was drawn to the fact that they weren't alcoves at all, but the entrances to tunnels, each fenced off with a padlocked grille.

It was Charles Chilton-Foliat. He held a golf-club in his hand but Linus had no difficulty in concluding that golf was not what was uppermost in his mind. In view of Mrs Egremont's condition, there was really only one possible explanation for Charles's presence but Linus had become so conditioned to thinking of George Upperby as the most likely candidate for murder that the truth did not immediately dawn on him.

'She's dead,' he said and then frowned. 'She didn't say anything about meeting you here.'

'She wasn't expecting to, but I didn't think it was a good idea for her to be wandering around in a place like this so I suggested she shelter in here. She seemed to think it was quite a good idea.'

'Wasn't it locked?'

'It was when I got here but Meriel's got a nice little part-time job here and she had the keys today because she'll be opening up in the morning.' He laughed. 'It'll give her quite a turn, don't you think?'

Linus smiled uneasily. 'I shouldn't think they'll allow it to be opened. The forensic people will have a lot to do here. By the time Meriel turns up it'll all be closed off.'

'I don't think you quite understand,' Charles told him. 'No one's going to know anything about it until morning.'

Linus looked at him in silence and frowned. 'What do you mean—no one's going to know? I don't know what you intend to do but I'm going to the first phone-box I can find to telephone the police.'

Charles shook his head. 'The only way you're leaving here, Rintoul, is along with Maud Egremont in a plastic bag.'

That was the moment when Linus realized he had been just a smidgeon stupid. 'You killed her,' he said.

'Well done, old man. Spot on. When she told us she couldn't come to supper because she had arranged to meet you here, I guessed she intended to change her will again and leave provision for the dogs to some charity or other. I couldn't risk that. You see, Meriel and I need the money. We need it rather badly, as a matter of fact. It was quite a blow to learn that she'd already changed it in such a way as to have made it scarcely worth all the effort I've been expending.'

'I'm not sure I follow,' Linus said. He was eyeing the ladder and playing for time. That ladder was the only way up that Linus knew of and as soon as an opportunity arose, he was going to take it and get away. The golf club and the state of Mrs Egremont's head suggested that the one had been used to effect the other. It therefore seemed reasonable that it was Chilton-Foliat's only weapon and it was one which could hardly be used to any effect once the intended victim's head was out of reach. Unfortunately, the man who was wielding it was standing at the foot of the ladder and it was hard to see how he could be coaxed away. Linus could only hope that by keeping him talking, time would relax Chilton-Foliat's guard.

'Didn't anyone tell you of the original provisions she made for her dogs? That her estate was to be divided among them and each dog, together with its share of the money, would go to its breeder? That if any of the breeders was dead, any dogs of their breeding, together with their portion of the estate, would go to whomever of the remaining breeders was prepared to look after them?'

'I'd heard something of the sort, though not the full details,' Linus admitted.

'Everyone in the breed knew about it. It was a bit of a joke—sell Mrs E. a dog and live in luxury for evermore, always assuming the dog outlived its owner. That's when I should have acted. I've been kicking myself for hanging back. When you came on the scene and hey presto, things were changed so that there was someone to oversee the welfare of the dogs and no capital until you were satisfied the dog had lived out its allotted span, I cursed the fact that even if you dropped dead the next day, the dogs we'd sold her would live, barring accidents, another seven or eight years before I could lay my hands on the capital.'

'Your hands?' Linus interrupted. 'I thought your wife was the breeder?'

'On paper, yes. In practice we work together but that's irrelevant: Meriel doesn't understand money. She always follows my advice. Anyway, I decided not to leave it to chance any more: I couldn't afford the risk that the dogs would die before their owner. Things were getting tight. That's why Meriel had to get a part-time job—mind you, that's turned out to be very useful. I wanted to get our hands on the dogs and if the other owners were dead, we'd stand to collect the lot eventually.'

Linus resisted the temptation to draw Charles's attention to the fact that his financial acumen didn't seem to be all that brilliant: goading him was probably not the wisest course of action, given their respective circumstances. 'So you set about killing them, is that it?' he asked instead.

'That's right. Janine Flatford was easy. I'd heard her invite Mrs E. to the theatre. All I had to do was bump into her as she came out and suggest a drink and a little walk. Then I made it look like a mugging gone wrong. Quite a clever stroke, that.'

'Yes, very,' Linus agreed. 'Why didn't you use it again? On Julian Treorchy?'

'I toyed with the idea. In fact, that was an attempt that wasn't entirely satisfactory. I decided I needed to get both of them because I couldn't be quite sure Ted wouldn't have a case for claiming the dog was bred in partnership—and anyway, they're both queers so the world would be better off without them. I'm not a great mechanic but I look after my own car and I'm more than capable of sabotaging brakes. It only takes half a minute and a dog show car park is virtually deserted around midday when everyone's at the show. Don't suppose you've ever thought of that.'

Linus agreed, mendaciously, that it was news to him.

'There you are, you see,' Charles said smugly. 'You have to plan things right and that means looking at all the angles. In fact, it was so empty that I had the chance to spray the car so that it looked like a straight case of queer-bashing.' He laughed. 'No pun intended but it's rather a good one don't you think?'

There were limits to Linus's preparedness to placate. 'Depends on what you mean by good,' he said. 'Clever, certainly, but tasteless.'

'Like all the best humour,' Charles said, unoffended. 'It was a detail I'd hoped to be able to include, which is why I had a spray-can with me. I was quite pleased to be able to do it. It added the finishing touch. Pity Ted managed to survive, though.'

'What were your plans for Sharon Dedham?' Linus asked.

'That was a problem. Of course, doctoring those brakes was doubly useful because, if the police got around to the dog connection, that frightful husband of hers would have been their first port of call—he's a car mechanic, you know.'

'Yes, I do know.'

'Couldn't use it again, though, and I didn't dare use the mugging. There was always the Korean Palace Dog connection between them—nothing I could do about that —so it was crucial there was nothing else to connect the cases. No, I was really stuck there for a while. It was sheer good luck that Kevin beat her to a pulp.'

'Not for Sharon,' Linus said drily.

Charles looked at him blankly for a moment, then a smile crept across his face. It wasn't a particularly pleasant smile. 'I do like a man with a sense of humour. Pity we couldn't have been on the same side,' he said.

'And so, with all the other breeders dead, all you had to do was get rid of Mrs Egremont,' Linus said. 'Pity you didn't know she'd completely changed her will and all those previous arrangements have gone—in my favour, I believe.'

Charles scowled and shifted the golf-club as if arranging its balance more comfortably. 'As a matter of fact, I did,' he said. 'That was thanks to Winifred. Stupid woman. I only had to show the slightest interest and she was eating out of my hand. I think she really believed that if she played her cards right, I'd leave Meriel for her.'

'Are you sure?' Linus said. 'She must be a good bit older than you.'

'Oh, she was. She used to call me her toy-boy. Enough to make you puke. She was at that silly age when they clutch at anything. I only put up with it because she was such a useful source of information. Under the last will, you ended up with most of the capital, Winifred got a tidier sum than previously, and anyone who took a dog back got a generous sum for its keep while it lived and a lump sum —quite a respectable sum, but nothing to compare with the original—when it was dead, provided you were satisfied that it hadn't been put down prematurely. When Winifred told me that she was changing it all over again, thanks to you, I knew I had to get rid of both of them before she could do it: this time the dogs and the bulk of the money were going to a charity, there was a bigger sum still for Winifred and you got a nice little windfall for all your advice.'

'How did Winifred know all this?'

'Mrs E. had given her some sort of a hint and George Upperby had a word with the family lawyer who'd drawn up the draft.'

'I thought she was going to change her solicitor,' Linus said.

'Don't know anything about that. The one she's got has been dealing with their affairs since the year dot. I dare say loyalty had a lot to do with it. She always set a lot of store by loyalty. Of course, that meant I had to act really quickly or risk losing everything. It was easy to get rid of Winifred, the only one who might be able to put two and two together, and that gave me the chance to persuade Meriel that it was our duty to be helpful friends to Mrs E. I was looking for the right opportunity and it came when she rang to say she couldn't come to supper because she was meeting you here. Not sure where your death will leave the estate, but at least we ought to come out of it modestly well.'

Hardly any light filtered down the shaft now. It must be almost dark. Both men's eyes had become accustomed to what light there was and Linus realized that there had been no slackening in Charles's vigilance. Then he bethought him of the only weapon he had—his torch.

It would be useless as a weapon in the usual sense of the word—one blow from the golf-club would dash it to the ground—but its light suddenly flashed in Charles's face just might be sufficiently strong after the steadily increasing dimness to which their eyes had adjusted to distract the man's attention long enough for Linus to make a dive at the ladder.

He slid his hand into his pocket and switched on the torch, knowing no glow would penetrate the waxed and lined pocket of his jacket. Then he stealthily withdrew his hand.

His strategy failed. He hadn't taken into account the fact that Chilton-Foliat must have known he had a torch; there might also have been something in the tenseness of his body that alerted the other man to the fact that he was preparing for something. Whatever the cause, the torch had no sooner emerged from his pocket than the golf-club swung out to knock it away.

Linus spun round, almost losing his balance—but not the torch. Now Charles was flailing about him with the club and in the confined space of the shaft Linus knew it was only a matter of time before blows rained down on his head. The ladder was out of the question: from his position at its foot, Charles's weapon could reach almost to the circumference of the shaft. There was no need for him to leave the foot of the ladder unprotected.

There was just one place through which escape might be effected: along the horizontal tunnels that radiated out from the central shaft. Such detail as Linus had unconsciously absorbed when he first came down here indicated that it would be impossible to stand up in them. It might not even be possible to crawl—and Linus hated confined spaces. On the other hand, it would be impossible for Charles to use his weapon if he came after Linus and if he didn't? Well, it would be a cold night but tomorrow was Saturday, a day when visitors could be expected. Charles might—probably would—stay in the shaft but he would have to be gone by morning. The first visitors would find Linus and Mrs Egremont's body, and he would have a lot of explaining to do. Linus smiled grimly to himself as he evaded the club once more. He might well have all night to plan a presentation of the truth which would be convincing.

On the whole, though, he thought Chilton-Foliat would follow him because the one thing of which Linus could be sure was that Mrs Egremont's murderer would not want him to get out alive.

He was a good bit older than Charles Chilton-Foliat and he could feel himself tiring. He couldn't keep up this dodging and darting much longer. He wished he had been here before. He had no idea whether the tunnels led into another shaft like this one; whether they were interlinked; or whether each led to a dead-end vein of flint. It didn't much matter. They were his only means of escape. He recalled that each entrance had been barred by a padlocked grille. He also recalled that Charles had emerged from one of them, which suggested that that padlock at least had been unlocked. He tried to remember which one it had been. He thought he knew but it was at best a gamble.

Linus timed it like an athlete. He ducked under the flailing club and into the alcove.

A wrench at the little gate told him the gods had been with him. He dived in and slammed it shut to delay his pursuer. It occurred to him that it might be a good idea to fasten the padlock. That way Charles's best bet would be to leave and put as much distance between him and Grimes Graves as he could before morning.

Then he remembered that Charles had the keys. That wouldn't work.

His instincts had been right: he couldn't even sit up straight and the tunnel soon became too low to allow him to crawl. The only way to progress was to lie on his front and slither along the dank, damp, slippery chalk. He kept his torch in his pocket. Its beam of light would have been a welcome companion but a treacherous one.

He heard the clang of iron behind him. He stopped and listened. It was followed by a sound he couldn't immediately identify which in turn was punctuated by grunts.

He was being followed.

Now what?

As he groped and wriggled his way through the tunnels he became aware that, while they were in fact quite wide, the roof became imperceptibly lower. Neolithic man was presumably lean to the point of gaunt. Linus wasn't. To his fundamental dislike of physically tight places was added the dread of becoming stuck and the fear that he had metaphorically painted himself into a corner. The further he went from the main shaft, the less light there was, until he was writhing along in total darkness.

That darkness and his unaccustomed mode of locomotion meant that he had no idea whether he had gone a few yards or several, whether the tunnel went in a straight line or a curve. From time to time he would find a natural pillar on one side or the other, presumably left by the original miners to prevent the roof falling in.

He wished he hadn't thought of that possibility. The mines had been here undisturbed for thousands of years— tens of thousands for all Linus knew—and only recently in their history had tourists been visiting them. What's more, if the metal gratings over the tunnel entrances were anything to go by, access beyond the main shaft had never been available. Linus could think of several reasons why this should be so. One of them was the possible instability of the roof. He stopped moving and closed his eyes as if by doing so he could blank out the picture he was conjuring up and he swallowed hard to fight back the rising nausea which was, he knew, due solely to fear. Then he opened his eyes and listened. If Charles Chilton-Foliat was still following him, he must be some way behind. Linus strained his ears. No, there wasn't total silence. There was still movement in the tunnels but how far away it was and at what speed it was moving, it was impossible to say. He slid his hand down to his pocket and felt the torch. Dared he

bring it out for a quick look around? Maybe. He decided
to risk it.

That was when real panic set in.

He could take his hand out of his pocket but he couldn't
raise his elbow that extra distance to bring out the torch
as well and when he tried to turn on his side to take advantage of the tunnel's width, he discovered that the height
was insufficient to accommodate the width of his shoulders.
He must stay on his front.

Think! he told himself. Think, man, think! Don't give in
to it. Take a deep breath. Take several. Then count slowly
up to ten and then think.

He could read the luminous dial of his wristwatch. Fine.
That meant he would know when the Graves were open
again. Graves! That was an unfortunate choice of word.
He would know when the place was open but how did he
find his way back to the main shaft? With a torch it might
have been possible. Charles Chilton-Foliat ceased to be a
menace. There was nothing he could do to Linus down
here.

When they opened up in the morning, they'd find Mrs
Egremont—and they'd find the unlocked grille. They'd see
the marks and presumably they'd send potholers in to
investigate. That was a comforting thought.

Unless, of course, Charles had got out and re-locked the
grille. Then no one would have any reason to look beyond
and Linus could be in here . . . The prospect was not one
upon which he wished to dwell.

Think! he told himself again. There has to be a way. All
you've got to do is think rationally and logically.

It wasn't easy and there was now no sound in the tunnels
except his own breathing, over which he seemed to have
very little control.

He made himself cast his mind back to the moment he
entered the tunnel. The main shaft had been circular which
meant that all the tunnels had radiated off. He recollected

that he had been bearing off to the left before the light faded. Presumably therefore, if he could go on bearing left, he would sooner or later see the faint light from the main shaft that would guide him back.

Always assuming neolithic man had hewn his tunnels in a roughly geometric pattern.

It was more probable that he had just followed the veins of flint.

In any case, it was night now. There wouldn't be any light.

All the same, he had to do something. He couldn't just lie here doing nothing. For all he knew he might be within feet of a grating.

For all you know, a little voice whispered, you might be half a mile away by now.

Linus pushed the thought resolutely away. He would keep on bearing left and whenever he felt a space on the left he would investigate to see if it led back to the shaft. It wasn't foolproof but he chose not to consider the flaws. He had to do something positive. Charles Chilton-Foliat and his murderous intent were suddenly no longer important. He could wait.

The trouble with reaching off to the left was that it was impossible to tell whether he had reached far enough and whether he was back where he had been before reaching out. Linus tried to time himself but that was only depressing—except for one thing: it convinced him that he was moving much more slowly than he had realized and that therefore perhaps he hadn't been so very far in, after all. This was the first optimistic thought to have crossed his mind and he held on to it with a tenacity that surprised him.

He found the grille by accident.

His head hit it.

It soon became clear that it wasn't the one by which he had entered or, if it were, then Charles Chilton-Foliat had already found it, got out and locked it behind him. That didn't matter. Linus knew now that all he had to do was to keep going round, reaching out every so often so that he didn't miss the end of the pillar separating one tunnel from another. That way he could examine each grille in turn and if Charles hadn't escaped, then the one they'd come in by would still be open.

It was a good thing for Linus's peace of mind that he was unaware that the chalk supports were not invariably pillars: one of them was a wall some twenty feet long and even some of the 'pillars' were irregular shapes of ten feet or more.

Linus was lucky. He found his second grille—and it was open.

With a sigh of relief he climbed out and closed it behind him.

He paused and listened.

Nothing. It was quite dark in the shaft but he could hear no breathing except his own. He held his breath. No, he was alone.

He took out his torch now and flashed it round the shaft. Mrs Egremont was still there but there was no sign of her killer. Linus made for the ladder.

Two steps up, he stopped. Not so fast, he thought. He went back to the grille. He had closed it but it wasn't locked. If Charles was still in there, Linus saw no good reason why he should be able to get out. He fastened the padlock. Charles had the keys, of course, but even if he found his way back to the shaft, finding the right key would add a further delay and Linus didn't intend to waste any time before calling the police.

When Linus was once more outside the little entrance building over the shaft, he fastened that padlock, too. It would be a simple matter for anyone who got that far to smash one of the windows and clamber through, but anything that might additionally delay Chilton-Foliot's escape was useful.

That done, he ran as quickly as he could over the uneven ground to the car park. Both his own car and Mrs Egremont's were still there, so, if Charles had already got out, he hadn't taken either of them. Linus recalled the car he had seen among the trees. He had taken it to belong to a courting couple. Now he wondered whether perhaps it had been Charles's. If that, too, were still there, it could only mean that the killer was still below ground. It was too far off to be visible. That was something the police could investigate.

Linus fished his car keys out of his pocket and started the engine. He remembered reading somewhere that there was a phone-box within three-quarters of a mile of every home in Britain. He doubted it but even if it were so, that was no guarantee it would be working and his instinct told him time was now of the essence.

As he drove down the track leading from the site, a picture flashed fuzzily into his mind. A house. Hadn't there been a house just where this track had turned off the road? He slowed down and then blessed his memory. He glanced at his watch. No wonder the house was in darkness. They wouldn't thank him for knocking them up. Tough.

A police car arrived very promptly indeed and it wasn't long before Detective-Inspector Rievaulx and his sergeant arrived.

'Our paths do seem to cross, Mr Rintoul,' he commented as he joined them at the padlocked entrance. He glanced at the lock. 'You fastened this?' he asked.

'To keep Chilton-Foliat down there. Or at least to slow up his escape.'

'I don't suppose you happen to have the keys?'

'No. Chilton-Foliat's got those and I think he's still down there.'

'Think?'

'It's conceivable he got out first. I think his was the car I saw parked over there. If it was and he has, then it won't be there now.'

'I don't suppose you know how he happened to come by the keys in the first place?'

'He told me he got them from his wife. She works here part-time and she was due to open up in the morning.'

Rievaulx nodded at one of the policemen. 'Force it,' he said. 'She was going to get a nasty shock when she did so, wasn't she?' he added conversationally. 'I don't think you need come down with us, Mr Rintoul. Just don't run away.'

A police Range-Rover arrived as he and his companions disappeared into the shaft and one of the policemen on board directed the ferocious beam of its spotlight down the opening. Linus went to the top of the ladder and peered down. The interior was brighter than it could ever have been in natural daylight. He wondered how far along the passages it could be seen.

The police were examining Mrs Egremont and Linus caught a glimpse of the golf-club lying on the ground. Did that mean Chilton-Foliat had escaped? Or had he abandoned it as useless when he had followed Linus in?

It was a long time before a rescue team got Charles Chilton-Foliat out. Like Linus, he had found the enclosed space more than he could bear. Unlike Linus, he had been unable to form a strategy to cope with it. The consequence was he had been petrified with fear and when they finally dragged him out, he was in too bad a mental state to help them in any way.

That abject, paralysing fear left him once he was back in the open air and saw Linus standing there, watching.

'That's him,' he said. 'That's the man who's done away with everyone who stood between him and that poor woman's fortune. Don't let him get away!'

'Don't worry, sir, Mr Rintoul will be accompanying us

in another car,' Inspector Rievaulx said soothingly. 'We shall want statements from both of you.'

Back at the station, Linus gave his account of events as dispassionately and accurately as he could, but as he drew to the end, his anxiety could no longer be hidden. 'The trouble is, Inspector, it's my word against his, and I've got at least as good a motive as he has. Some might say better.'

'Very true, Mr Rintoul, but we don't depend just on that, you know. Do you recall whether you handled the golf-club?'

'I didn't. I'm quite sure of that.'

'Do you recall whether Mr Chilton-Foliat was wearing gloves?'

Linus thought back. 'I don't think so. Not when I saw him.'

'Then I think we can leave it to forensic to rule you out even if it isn't necessarily conclusive evidence against Mr Chilton-Foliat. Then there's the fact that you didn't kill him to prevent his trying to incriminate you, you called the police instead of getting as far away as possible—and it would have been very easy to get on a ferry and be in Holland before Mrs Egremont was found—and then, having called us, you waited around for us to arrive. This might only prove that you're exceptionally cunning. I suspect, however, that it's an indication of a clear conscience.' He shuffled his papers. 'I gather Mrs Egremont's death makes you a very rich man.'

'So everyone gives me to understand, and all on account of those blasted dogs. Heaven alone knows what I'm going to do with them. You've seen where I live, Inspector— where do I put half a dozen dogs? Not to mention the annoyance they'll cause. They're a pretty yappy breed.'

'If things are left the way it seems likely, you'll be able to move into their old home.'

Linus snorted. 'It's a long way to cycle to work, Inspector. No, I'll see about setting up some sort of trust fund to look after them. There must be some way out of it.'

'In the meantime, would you like me to book you into a hotel? We'd like you to be around for a few days.'

'I'd appreciate it,' Linus said. He glanced down at himself for the first time since he came out of the shaft. His clothes were liberally streaked with damp chalk. 'If I turned up looking like this and with no luggage, I think they'd be full up.'

Inspector Rievaulx grinned. 'You have a point. I'll get a car to drop you round and vouch for you. As my old father would have said, you look as if you need to see a man about a dog.'

Linus grimaced. 'Very droll, Inspector. Don't call us, we'll call you.'

He could hear the Inspector chuckling as he went to order a car.